D1480933

CONTEMPORARY RUSSIAN FICTION

A SHORT LIST

Russian Authors Interviewed by Kristina Rotkirch

Editors:
Anna Ljunggren,
Kristina Rotkirch

Translated by Charles Rougle

The publication of this book
was supported by Stockholm University.

GLAS PUBLISHERS
tel./fax: +7(495)441-9157
perova@glas.msk.su
www.russianpress.com/glas

DISTRIBUTION

in North America
NORTHWESTERN UNIVERSITY PRESS
Chicago Distribution Center
tel: 1-800-621-2736 or (773) 702-7000
fax: 1-800-621-8476 or (773) 702-7212
pubnet@202-5280
www.nupress.northwestern.edu

in the UK
INPRESS LIMITED
tel: 020 8832 7464; fax: 020 8832 7465
mail1@inpressbooks.co.uk
www.inpressbooks.co.uk

Within Russia
JUPITER-IMPEX
www.jupiters.ru
shop@jupiters.ru

ISBN 978-5-7172-0084-4

CONTENTS

FOREWORD

"Contemporary literature" is a shifting concept. Like the words "already" and "still" and "I" and "you," what is contemporary is relative to the speaker and commensurate to our own lives within the culture. The idea for the present book was conceived three years ago in Stockholm as part of a larger research project. Since then Russian literature has moved forward with the publication of such works as Vladimir Sorokin's *Day of the Oprichnik* (*Den oprichnika,* Zakharov; 2006), Victor Pelevin's *Empire V (Ampir V,* Eksmo; 2006) and Ludmila Ulitskaya's *Daniel Stein, Interpreter* (*Daniel Shtain, perevodchik,* Eksmo; 2006; and there is also a major forthcoming novel by Mikhail Shishkin. Today it is quite clear that the cultural period that began with perestroika is over, and this decade and a half may soon come to be considered as an interval marked by a relative power vacuum with regard both to institutions and to prevailing aesthetic values. The dissemination of unofficial pre-perestroika culture is complete, and the pressure of the commercial mass market is increasing. At the same time, Soviet culture has become more distant and no longer serves as an effective aesthetic counterweight or negative reference point for "real" culture, thereby weakening the iconoclastic impact of literature connected with conceptualism, which made wide use of "Soviet" material. The assimilation and vigorous development of the postmodernist experience is colliding with the "strong" authorial voice typical of Russian literature and has evidently passed its zenith. What is needed is a new aesthetics, or at least a new target. Given today's rather unstable cultural panorama, any selection of authors is arguable. We hope, however, that the writers we have chosen are fairly representative of the variety in contemporary Russian literature and that readers will recognize all their names and find their opinions interesting. Something curious we discovered when all the interviews had been conducted: one group of authors was in various ways involved with translation (Petrushevskaya, Akunin, Pelevin, and Shishkin), while another — Grishkovets, Sadur, and again Petrushevskaya — came from the theater. This seems to suggest that verbal imitation and stylization have been an important impulse in the evolution of contemporary prose. The extensiveness of this stylizing tendency accounts for the great interest in documentary and memoir literature and predetermines the direction of the quest for a new aesthetics.

A few words about the preparation of the present book. The starting point was an evening devoted to contemporary Russian prose in the newly opened Nobel Museum in Stockholm in 2001. This discussion gave rise to the research project "Contemporary Russian Prose: Traditions, Anti-Traditions, New Aesthetics" at the Department of Slavic Languages and Literatures at Stockholm University and in collaboration with Nikolai Bogomolov and Oleg Lekmanov of the Department of Journalism at Moscow State University. Biographical introductions and photographic materials were prepared by Vadim Radetsky.

With the exception of Viktor Pelevin's and Ludmila Ulitskaya's written answers and Ludmila Petrushevskaya's response in the form of an essay, the book is based on conversations with the writers. With support from the Swedish Foundation for Culture in Finland and the Magnus Bergwall Foundation in Sweden, the interviews were conducted by

Kristina Rotkirch, Finland-based Swedish translator, journalist, and publisher of a series of contemporary Russian novels in Sweden and Finland. The Granholm Foundation (Stockholm University) and Vera Sager's Foundation have supported translation into English and publication.

Anna Ljunggren

TRANSLATOR'S NOTE

Transliteration of Russian words follows J. Thomas Shaw's system. Titles of works are given in transliteration followed by a translation in parentheses when they first occur in the text, with the English title only in subsequent references. Works that have appeared in English translation use those titles. All others are my own.

Charles Rougle

Interviews with
Russian Authors

Boris AKUNIN
(Grigory Chkhartishvili)

"Boris Akunin is first and foremost a project related to the status of mass culture."

Boris Akunin, a pseudonym derived from a Japanese word meaning approximately "outlaw," is the pen name of writer, literary scholar, and translator Grigory Shalvovich Chkhartishvili. He was born on 20 May 1956 in Georgia. His father was in the military, and his mother was a teacher of Russian language and literature. He has lived in Moscow since he was two years old, and is a graduate of the History and Philology Department of the Institute of Asian and African Studies at Moscow State University. His translations from Japanese and English include works by Yukio Mishima, Yasushi Inoue, Kôbô Abe, T. Coragessan Boyle, Malcolm Bradbury, and Peter Ustinov.

Akunin is best known for his Erast Fandorin mysteries. His first literary work was the novel *Azazel* in this series, which appeared in April 1998, followed by *The Turkish Gambit* (*Turetsky gambit*). Besides the Fandorin series, he has authored the series *The Adventures of Sister Pelagia* (*Priklyucheniya sestry Pelagii*), *The Adventures of the Master* (*Priklyucheniya magistra*), and *Genres* (*Zhanry*).

He is the author of *The Writer and Suicide* (*Pisatel i samoubiistvo*; Moscow: Novoe literaturnoe obozrenie; 1999, 2006) and is also known for his literary criticism. From 1999 through 2000 he was deputy editor of the journal *Inostrannaya literatura*, editor-in-chief of the twenty-volume *Anthology of Japanese Literature* (*Antologiya yaponskoy literatury*), and chairman of the board of the major publishing project "Pushkin Library" (Pushkinskaya biblioteka). During the last years Akunin has also written a number of plays.

Looking back on it now, how do you yourself view the birth of your hero Erast Fandorin? In other words, how did you become a writer?

As I see it, everything connected with the "project" Boris Akunin is an amazingly un-Russian literary phenomenon, beginning with the word "project", which in reference to literature sounds rather blasphemous, or at least unpleasant. Because in Russia literature is something that comes not from the head but from the heart, from that Russian soul that in reality evidently doesn't exist. As for me, I'd like everything to come from the head, whence the "project." Ten years have passed and the word "project" has already been worn bare, but back then in '97 when all of this started, it sounded rather provocative. So it's something invented from beginning to end, thought up, architecturally constructed. First came the conception, the idea, that is, something theoretical, and then this concept began taking on certain theoretical features. In general, at first I wasn't thinking of this idea as a writer, but as an editor. I didn't intend to write all this, I intended to organize it.

Like Rembrandt, for others later?

Not so much Rembrandt but Diaghilev. Like an impresario, I wanted to do the organizing, and my friends and acquaintances, who include a lot of talented writers, would do the writing. As for me, at the time not only was I not a prosaist but I had no intention of becoming one. I was a philologist, an essayist, a literary critic. It was clear to me that something like this had to come along in Russia. There was a demand for it; readers expected it. A new category of readers had appeared that hadn't existed before, and they needed reading matter that hadn't existed before. We can very conditionally call it entertaining reading for the educated, cultured reader, something we didn't have here at all. It appeared in Europe ten or fifteen years earlier, the most vivid examples being Umberto Eco or Patrick Süsskind. Then later there is Baricco in Italy. Before that, Calvino. It's postmodernist literature. Entertaining, yet not *shamefully* so — entertaining literature on a rather high intellectual level. In the mid-90s popular literature in Russia presented a wretched spectacle. It was dominated by pulp fiction of the worst kind. Or people read translated American trash, which is even more primitive. Meanwhile a new class was taking shape in Russia, known here as the "middle class," although it differs considerably from the European middle class. Nevertheless, it was a class of people who needed all the appropriate attributes: its own ethics, its own aesthetics, and its own culture, including its own entertaining literature. At first I tried to persuade my friends to write in this genre. I failed, because as befits Russian writers, most of them are talented but lazy. Finally I decided to begin by doing a kind of prototype of the genre to show what it might look like. I'll demonstrate the technique, I thought, the public will be overjoyed, writers will catch it on the fly, and after that it will be easy. I wrote the first novel under a pseudonym, because this was a rather risky undertaking for a person in literary circles who worked for a respectable literary journal. That sort of scribbling was considered unbecoming of a serious scholar. I published *Azazel* in 1998, and it didn't sell at all, so there was nothing for me to brag about and nothing I could demonstrate. Evidently, my idea wasn't working. Still, I was sure I was right, and besides that, writing the novel gave me unexpected and very intense pleasure. It was remarkable: I would write after work, in the evening, I don't know — in the train, during breaks. It was a pure, unadulterated return to adolescence, a remarkable game. So I wrote a second novel, and a third, and a fourth...

And suddenly...

Not suddenly. The explosion didn't come until the fifth book. First the critics started writing about me, then people started buying, and then I came into vogue. It was just at the right time. I was more successful than these books deserved, because the timing was right. That's how it all began.

So your explanation of your enormous success is just that the timing was right?

I was lucky in that the expectations of the public coincided with my inner need. You cannot successfully make such a product if it doesn't interest you. It really took hold of me. I'm still interested in it, and I constantly discover in genre literature intriguing new possibilities.

How was it for you as a representative of the Moscow intelligentsia to become a representative of popular culture? Today it's said that you are more of a "brand" than a writer. Do you find that insulting?

No, I'm very happy about it. This project was interesting to me in various senses. What I've been talking about so far has to do with cultural strategy — creating a new genre of reading, which by and large did not yet exist in Russia. But there is also a literary point of view. It is interesting to work with different styles, trends, and genres. I was also intrigued by the business aspect, no doubt about it. I wanted to create a situation in which the author is not an entity dependent on a literary agent or publishing house or movie studio. Instead, the author would conduct this entire orchestra. From the beginning I knew that I would have several publishers and several agents, and that I would never sell the exclusive rights to a screen version. I managed to do all this. Besides, during the 90s I got tired of my intellectual friends' whining and complaining, their moaning that they couldn't make ends meet, that no one needed their cultural baggage, that in today's awful society intellectuals cannot be successful. This is not true. I wanted to show that without making any compromises and doing what interests you and gives you pleasure you can be successful, and that you don't even have to take away anyone else's place in the sun.

Most of your novels are set in the latter half of the nineteenth century. Why have you chosen that particular period?

Because it interests me. Why? It helps me to understand the present day in Russia. There are many parallels between Alexander II's reforms and Alexander III's reactionary policies on the one hand, and the period of Yeltsyn's reforms and Putin's reaction, on the other. We remember how those perturbations ended, and there is the danger that contemporary Russia will repeat the same mistakes. It's important to me to think about such questions and to force readers to think about them. Let them compare and draw conclusions. That's one reason. Secondly, I just like this period aesthetically. It's the period of Art Nouveau, when manual and machine labor come together. I really love artifacts from this period because the first technical innovations were still being made by hand, and each one of them had its individuality.

The telephone…

The revolver, everything. In addition, I truly feel a kind of nostalgia for the spirit of that time, when it seemed that all problems could be solved with the help of energy, will, and reason, that very soon there would be a paradise on earth, because it would become possible to build a proper society. Machines would fly through the air, and everyone would be well fed and clothed and happy. Today we know that happiness is structured differently but I feel certain nostalgia for Chernyshevsky's heroics. It was a time when human life seemed simpler than it does now.

Besides the period, in the Fandorin novels the city of Moscow is important.

Very much so. Moscow is my city. I've lived here all my life and I have a good sense of it. I can't say that I like it but I truly do love it. I see Moscow differently because I know its history. I see streets and buildings but showing through the glass and concrete I also see the contours of buildings that used to be there. I have a good idea of the history of Moscow's streets. I'm in general interested in very old large cities standing on a very thick cultural stratum, because when you start digging up a street a foot and a half down you find cobblestones; in another foot and a half the road is paved with wood; even deeper you can see the stone vaults of a basement, or a house that once stood here, and so on and so forth. An old city is such a special place.

Your next project was the Provincial Detective series. It is also set in the late nineteenth century, but in different environs — a small provincial town and particularly the Orthodox church. Why did you leave Moscow?

I didn't leave it. These things were written in parallel, at the same time. I simply decided that the Fandorin cycle consists of adventure novels of a masculine cast, and I wanted to try and write a "feminine" novel made quite differently. It would be feminine in manner and intended mainly for women. The principal difference there is that in a "masculine" novel the outcome and the "why" of it are most important, whereas in a "feminine" novel the most important thing is the "how": the process of reading is more important than the result. There should be more pleasure from reading itself — sensuous pleasure — than from solving a mystery. And I wanted to contrast the Yin and Yang as much as possible. As for the Yin, not only is the heroine a woman, not only does she rely more on her intuition than on logic, but the tempo is different, the style is different; and, moreover, it was necessary to contrast the capital and the provinces because the provinces represent a feminine principle — enfolding, supple, more vital. It is contrasted to the logical, rigid, inert center. This same feminine principle is what interests me in the church because this pair — the State and the Church — are quite obviously the Yang and the Yin.

So you are now an expert on Orthodoxy?

I've read quite a lot about Orthodoxy, but my books should not be considered a collection of precise information about it. That was never my intention. Also, the Orthodoxy and priests

I portray are products of my imagination — I'm not out after accuracy. Instead, it's my idea of what Russian Orthodoxy could be, of what I would like it to be.

Were there any reactions on the part of the Church?

Well, not as an institution. I hope that the Orthodox Church has drawn some lessons from its history. We all remember how it anathemized Lev Tolstoy. I am not Lev Tolstoy, of course, but I hope the Orthodox Church will not be again censoring literature anytime soon. So far it has not. As for individual priests and believers, yes, many of them were irritated and even took offense at *Sister Pelagia and the Red Rooster (Pelagiya i krasny petukh)*. There was no reason to be insulted, because I in no way wanted to offend the feelings of believers. This book was written not for them, but for agnostics like myself.

I'm sure that many people experience nostalgic pleasure when they read about the Russia "we have lost." But aren't you idealizing the history of the country? The role of the regime, for example — one recalls how faithfully Erast Petrovich serves the tsar.

I'm often told this, and it surprises me each time because in my books there is no nostalgia for the empire, none whatever. There is nostalgia for the Russian literature of the period because it was remarkably capable of ennobling everything it saw and everything it described without in any way obscuring or concealing the vile, filthy aspects of Russian reality. There isn't the slightest trace of nostalgia for Russia's great power status. I portray the tsarist regime with little sympathy, and for that reason monarchists resent me. That the series is made up of various sub-genres of the detective story is another matter. *Azazel*, for example, is a romantic whodunit and therefore everything seems very romantic, but there is also the political mystery *The State Counsellor* (*Statsky sovetnik*) about terrorists and gendarmes, and it's unclear which are worse.

You're an historian by training. How important to you is historical accuracy? Or do you play with history as you wish?

I regard historical truth only as a background. It is important to me when I am collecting material for a novel, when I have to know what actually happened and all opinions about it. After that I write my own novel and do everything in my own way. Historical accuracy is limited to secondary details that create a feeling of verisimilitude, but I am not writing chronicle novels. My novels belong to the Alexander Dumas genre.

I remember especially clearly the last remarks of the Turk Anvar in **The Turkish Gambit**, *where he severely condemns Russia as an "unstable, absurd country" in which "savage destructive forces are fermenting that sooner or later will burst forth into the open"…*

I think that in many respects he is right and that the events of the twentieth century have borne him out. At the same time, however, his opponent — my heroine — is also right when she tries to argue with him. She says some illogical and silly things but they can't simply be brushed aside. "What about Russian literature?" she prattles. "What about Count Tolstoy and Dostoyevsky?" He replies, reasonably, that literature is something secondary. Switzerland, for example, has no great literature but it's a leading country and everyone there is free and lives well. He is right, and so is she, because in Russia, besides the tradition of despotism and aggression on the part of the state and the imperialist conquest of neighboring territories, there are also other values and other traditions. This is the Russia that interests me. This is the Russia, let's say, that I love. In addition, to me as an historian, Russia is of interest because it has the ability to change very rapidly and because I sense in it a mighty energy that is sometimes destructive but may also be creative. Add to that its size and expanse…

So it's an interesting place to live.

Absolutely. There were times when it was very boring. I remember it well. Reagan was wrong when he called the Soviet Union the "Evil Empire." The Soviet Union was an empire of monstrous boredom. It was unbearably boring here, especially if you were young and wanted to do something creative. Moscow was gray and boring. An utterly dead city. I simply hated it back then. But then time began moving and Moscow changed completely. For anyone who wants to do something it became perhaps the best city on earth. Russia, of course, remains in many respects a savage, cruel country that constantly tries you and practically every day puts you to some kind of test. On the other hand, however, it is a country in which you can achieve a great deal in a short time, in a wide variety of senses. It is a country in which new, exciting things are taking place. You live and feel that the earth is trembling beneath your feet. You don't know what will open up — a geyser, an earthquake, a volcano, or a fissure. You never know what to expect.

You've begun writing about today's Russia in Fairy-Tales for Idiots (Skazki dlya idiotov) and in Adventures of the Master (Priklyucheniya magistra) novel series. The picture of Russia there is not exactly positive.

We have enough writers who want to describe Russia in saccharine, syrupy tones. All you have to do is turn on the television. I have not set out to photograph reality. When I describe contemporary Russia it is sometimes a grotesque, sometimes a cartoon. Many critics have therefore accused me of Russophobia, which is not true. Even when I parody Russia I try to show it as it really is. At any rate, this is how I see it, with all the good and the bad mixed up together.

These texts are very entertaining on the verbal level as well. There was humor earlier, of course, as for example in the excellent story "The Jack of Spades" ("Pikovy valet") but it seems to me now your humor has become a more important element in your novels.

What can I offer of interest to readers when I write about contemporary life? After all, they are also living today and have the same amount of information as I do, and they have their own opinions. All I can offer them is my own view, painted in the colors that I find natural. Many things in present-day reality amuse me. Many things make me angry. I try to convey all this in an accessible way.

You said that people have reacted by calling you a Russophobe. Why?

The most common error is to equate the speech and opinions of the characters with the opinions of the author. This happens all the time — some character of mine says something negative about Russia and immediately people assume that it is my point of view. I became accustomed long ago to being accused of things that are mutually exclusive. I'm accused of being a monarchist and of hating the Russian tsar; of being a Russophobe and a Russia Firster. Recently I was in Poland. I was struck by the fact that at every meeting

I was asked why I disliked Poles so much. "Why do you say that?" I asked. "Well, look — here's an unattractive Pole and there's another one." I looked and yes, they were right. But it wasn't because I disliked Poles, it just happened that way. Then I began to protest: wait, there's a likeable Polish woman. I stopped there because I realized that this wasn't the proper level of discussion... What surprises me most of all is when people start accusing me of this or that political prejudice. Books are something apart, but I make no secret of my political views. I deliberately avoid issuing political declarations because I am a writer, not a politician, but when journalists ask me about something I give straight answers. You don't have to go looking in my novels for hidden opinions. Everything is out in the open.

In **Altyn-Tolobas** *the Englishman Nicholas Fandorin, Erast's grandson, comes to Russia for the first time and we see Moscow through the eyes of a naïve foreigner. This is quite a rewarding approach...*

That's right. It enables you to look at your own country from the outside, through the eyes of a stranger. At the same time, this Nicholas who comes to Russia understands nothing here and behaves very foolishly. This is a parody of people in my circle, Soviet intellectuals who have grown up here and have felt like aliens from outer space, alien bodies, their entire life. I remember very well the sensation of living in a country where everything is hostile toward you, from the authorities and official culture down to the interests and moods of the overwhelming majority of the population. It was like that. Then it began to change. Russia has changed enormously in the past twenty years. Personally, for example, I don't feel as though I belong to some sort of insignificant minority. If at the time of the South Korean airline incident Russia seemed to be a sinister place where nothing was going to happen, today I don't think so. I think that it makes sense to fight for Russia. Why, strictly speaking, should she be what our "hawks" want?

On another level, this theme of cultural contrasts is an important and constant theme of yours. We find it in almost all the Fandorin novels, which compare not only Russian and English culture, but also French, Japanese, German, Turkish... This is quite amusing, but surely it also contains something serious? You seem to be discovering Russian civilization through other cultures.

Russia is a big country, and it isn't mono-ethnic but has been subjected to very different cultural influences for a very long time. When characters in my novels set in the nineteenth century appear with German, Polish, Estonian surnames, I am not distorting anything. Almost a third of the population of St Petersburg, for example, were Lutherans. Half of the gentry were of non-Russian extraction. As for my authorial arbitrariness, I probably force the oriental element too much, simply because I am a Japanist and because I like it. It seems to me that Russia could use a healthy dose of the East. It's often said that we don't have enough of the West, but I would add that we lack the East, by which I mean the East in its best manifestations: its philosophy, mentality, aesthetics, ethics...

You have also worked as a translator...

Yes, I worked for several years translating Japanese literature into Russian.

Is there any connection between translation and what you are writing now?

I think so. In the first place, literary translation is an excellent school in which to master the profession of writing, to learn to feel comfortable with any style. I can easily imitate the literary signature tune of any writer. This adds yet another layer to my books.

The result is a literary detective genre. Besides the usual intrigue, the well-read reader is presented with an additional puzzle — recognizing the characters, situations, and styles of various authors.

I'm very fond of playing with allusions or "remakes." Sometimes a critic will up and unmask me: "Look, look, this is from Leskov, from his novel *Cathedral Folk.* I recognized it!" Well, of course. How could you not recognize it when I say at the beginning of the book that it is dedicated to N. S. This is Leskov, Nikolai Semenych. When intelligent critics discover an allusion they behave more delicately. They begin to examine it to find out what I've changed, how I've played with the situation and why and where Leskov has suddenly become Dostoyevsky, and Dostoyevsky has become Chekhov.

But this is probably lost when your works are translated into other languages.

Well, in Leskov's case, of course, it is lost, because he is not well known outside Russia. As for Dostoyevsky and Chekhov, I think that it is not entirely lost, since in many countries they have been translated many times and are recognizable. To the well-read reader their characters are also recognizable. Also, the allusions and quotations in my books come not only from Russian literature but from world literature as well.

What do you think when you read or hear about

reactions to your books abroad? Are they less well understood there?

Yes, of course, not to mention the fact that now every translated work belongs to the translator almost to the same degree as it belongs to me. The words are no longer mine but the words of the translator, words that have passed through him or her. Because I myself have worked as a literary translator I understand very well the extent to which the fate of a book in a different country depends on whether or not the author and the translator fit each other. Naturally, something is lost. But the main thing in a book is not the plot but how the words are combined, whether or not they produce a certain music. The words in a translation are different and they are combined differently. The result is a completely different music. If you've been lucky with your translator, this music is not worse than the music you wrote but it's a different music all the same.

Your latest "literary project" is **The Genres** *— a kind of collection of typical examples of various genres, such as* **The Children's Book, The Spy Novel,** *and so on. What do you have in mind — is this postmodernist play with the Soviet myth?*

It certainly is postmodernist. Everything I write is the purest postmodernism, if only because the sum of my knowledge and my entire experience are drawn not so much directly from life but from my reading of other books. My books are best read by well-read persons who have a certain competence. *The Genres* is an old idea of mine. I've long wanted to publish a new series in which the most diverse genres of mass literature would be represented, each in its purest form — more precisely, my idea of what each genre should look like. To begin with, I published three books simultaneously. The title of each book in this series is the name of the genre: the children's book is entitled *The Children's Book* (*Detskaya kniga*), the spy novel *The Spy Novel* (*Shpionsky roman*), and then there is *The Science Fiction Novel* (*Fantastika*). Perhaps I'll write *The Romance Novel* (*Lyubovny roman*), *The Historical Novel* (*Istori-chesky roman*), *The Production Novel* (*Proizvodstvenny roman*)[1], and so on.

As for detective fiction, why has it become so popular in Russia? Even by "real" writers such as Umberto Eco?

First of all, there is a lot of detective fiction everywhere. Here the genre is even more popular than in Europe or America, because Russia today, for one thing, is a more criminal country. There are more crimes committed here and more punishments. The theme is closer to real life. For another, it's a genre that did not exist at all in the Soviet period. As a new genre it arouses a certain interest. Fifteen years ago there simply was no Russian detective fiction. I think that's the reason.

What do you yourself read for pleasure?

By and large I don't read any fiction. Memoirs, diaries, history books, biographies — that's my usual reading. I like books on material culture.

What are you reading at the moment, if I may ask? What do you take along with you on the train?

Strange as it may seem, on the train I read fiction — Nabokov, for example, but in fact not for pleasure but for work.

---

[1] The Soviet production novel focused on depictions of industry or agriculture. Especially after the introduction of the first Five-Year Plan in the late 1920s, it became a standard genre of Socialist Realism.

But perhaps you get some pleasure as well?

I'm not a great fan of Nabokov.

Why do you need it for your work, then?

Well, I need to look at some of his stylistic peculiarities. Just now I'm reading Boris Slutsky's[2] memoirs about the war — very informative reading. Before that I read the memoirs of Sergei Solovyov, the poet and Uniate priest, grandson of the historian. Since I write fiction myself it's interesting to see how people describe real events, which I then transform into fiction.

What do you think about the film versions of your novels?

I'm fine with them. Film versions are a very useful way to get readers to buy more of your books.

That's all?

That's the main and the only use of a film version. What else could there be?

You also write for the theater?

Yes, a play of mine just came out — actually, two plays. They are entitled *Yin* and *Yang* and were written for the Russian Youth Theater. It's been running there for a year already. And now I've finally published it in book form. It's about Erast Fandorin and exists in two variants: one in white and the other in black — the Yin variant and the Yang variant. The same situation is played out differently, and the plays run on different days: today the white one, tomorrow the black one, and once a month back to back — a long play that begins at three in the afternoon and runs until evening.

---

[2] Boris Abramovich Slutsky (1919-1986) — poet and translator, author of several books of poetry, much of which remained unpublished in his lifetime.

Do you like the production?

Yes, it's a very successful performance. Even though I must add that I'm not awfully fond of the theater. I like the director Aleksey Borodin, who staged *Azazel* and these two plays. And audiences like it too. It's a large theater — 800 seats — and it's always full.

Now to my last questions. The Russian intelligentsia was traditionally in opposition to the regime. In this respect Erast Fandorin is an exception. What about yourself?

Erast Fandorin is not an exception, not at all. He is a man not of a Samurai but of a Confucian cast. The Samurai serves the ruler while the Confucian serves the cause. Erast Fandorin serves the State as long as his ideas of good and evil do not come into conflict with the State's ideas of good and evil. When that happens Erast Petrovich leaves the service and is even forced to leave the country for a time because the authorities and the government become hostile toward him. He cannot do otherwise. Confucius says: "The noble man serves his master until his service comes into conflict with his conscience."

Are you yourself a Samurai?

No, I'm not a Samurai because I have no master, and I'm not a Confucian because the Confucian serves a cause, and since I don't know of any cause that I would like to serve I just live for my own sake.

In the fall of 2006 you were targeted by the campaign against Georgian citizens in Moscow. Has this affected your attitude towards the state and your willingness to comment upon its actions?

Certainly. My view of the Putin regime has become significantly more negative. It's not only that this incident was hard on me because it temporarily interrupted my usual work schedule. I am alarmed by the direction in which our society is moving. I can't rule out the possibility that in the near future Russia may once again be facing serious ordeals.

Evgeny GRISHKOVETS

"I insist that what I write is literature based not on observation, but on emotional experience."

Evgeny Valerievich Grishkovets was born on 17 February 1967 in Kemerovo (Siberia). In 1984 he enrolled in the Department of Philology at Kemerovo University, the following year he was drafted and served for three years in the Pacific Fleet. After his discharge he returned to the university to finish his studies. There he performed pantomime at the student theater.

In 1990, at Kuzbas Engineering University, Grishkovets organized "The Loge," a student theater based on the principle of collective improvisations that staged some ten performances in seven years.

In 1998, he moved to Kaliningrad, and in November of that year staged his first one-man play *How I Ate a Dog* (*Kak ya syel sobaku*), which was first performed for 17 spectators in the smoking-room of the snack bar at the Russian Army Theater. In 1999 he was awarded the Anti-Booker Prize for his plays *Notes of a Russian Traveler* (*Zapiski russkogo puteshest-vennika*) and *Winter* (*Zima*). In 2000, he received two Golden Mask Awards in the categories "Innovation" and the "Critics' Prize", and also the national "Triumph" Award.

In the past few years Grishkovets has become widely known. In 2004 he was awarded the Book of the Year Prize for his novel *The Shirt (Rubashka)*. His book *Rivers (Reki)* came out in 2005 followed in 2006 by a book of short stories *The Mark (Planka)*. At the radio play festival in Vienna a German production of *How I Ate a Dog* won the first three prizes.

In 2002, together with the group "Bigudi", Grishkovets recorded his first music album *Now (Seychas)*, an unusual project on the interstices of literature, theater, music, and contemporary club culture. A second album, *To Sing (Pet)* followed in November 2004.

Evgeny Grishkovets defines himself professionally as an actor, director, producer, and writer.

———————

Let's talk first about your plays, which can easily be read as artistic prose. How do you yourself look upon your works now in retrospect?

My very first prose work was a transcribed text of my already existing play *How I Ate a Dog*. Today I regard it as archaic and in many respects a compromise, although I did try to write it according to literary rules and not as a verbatim record of the play. Then I wrote three plays that I think can very well be read as belles-lettres since there are almost no spoken lines and the text is easy, by which I mean it's not overloaded with stage directions. Once I had written a novel, however, the plays didn't interest me very much any more. In any case, I realize that when I write a play I'm always thinking of the theater, and that a play is incomplete as a work of literature. I write it as something not entirely finished because a play doesn't become a completed work of art until it has been performed in a theater. Moreover, it won't be my work any more but something done by someone else — the director is the author of the performance, for which he merely uses my play. What I've written and continue to write today, however, is intended for publication in book form and the only way you can become acquainted with it is to buy and read the book. Just now I'm in constant contact with people, traveling to cities in which my plays have never been staged, where I'm known only as a writer. Some people who have read *The Shirt* or *Rivers* become interested in what I'm doing in the theater and go to see my play and some of them like it much less. As for those who first saw me on the stage, they think that what I'm doing in literature is derivative. That's OK.

Still, you began as a playwright, and performing your own texts on stage must have influenced your style, hasn't it? Did your literary style evolve as a result of this process?

Yes. In the first place, because I did a lot of performances, I learned a lot of things about the people for whom I'm doing this — much more than other writers can. I met daily with hundreds of people who had watched me and this has had a powerful influence on my writing. My works contain no opinions at all about the world. I don't say what I like or don't like. This is a law of the theater, because the audience consists of hundreds of people with very different educations and social status, very different political views, and so on, and they are all watching the play at the same time. I have learned to speak to them all, and I've brought this universal mode of expression into literature. I've been accused of sounding excessively optimistic and life-asserting. This optimism comes from the theater, and in this sense when I read works by people of my age or younger I realize that I am radically different from them for the simple reason that I don't write about any social ills, I don't express any opinions about the present, of the country, or other people, or politics, and so on. I don't express any opinions at all. Opinions, after all, are very difficult to integrate into literature and art in general. Opinions are a private matter.

You seem to be particularly close to your heroes.

My heroes strongly resemble me because I'm not very good at inventing and thinking up things or eavesdropping on other people. Generally speaking, I only write about what I've personally experienced or know or what happened near me or has strongly affected me. For that reason my heroes resemble me and identify with me. I probably don't know how to do it differently. I am not a universal writer. I write only about what I've experienced, and because you can't experience a lot in a short period, I write fairly little.

*The characters in many of your works — the play **The City (Gorod)** or your novel **The Shirt**, for example — are representatives of the Moscow middle class. They are not very "Russian," however — you could find such people in any large European city. Or what do you think?*

Well, yes... I've also done quite a few performances in Europe, and when I was doing the first one I realized that I wasn't interested in telling the audience a "Russian" story about Russians. I very much want to tell a story about ordinary modern city dwellers. Not particularly Europeans but just generally ordinary. Details and facts about specific cities are not as important as what large Russian and European cities have in common. Purely Russian details could seriously distract a European reader, not to mention a theater audience, and since I am used to performing in the theater I know for a fact that people go there to hear something about themselves, not about some Russian guy from Siberia. That is why I have begun universalizing my texts by making them as detailed as possible but at the same time trying to select details that are universal to all Europeans whether they live in Helsinki or Nice.

Still, you are not writing for Western Europe!

Of course not. I write in Russian and for the Russian reader, on the assumption that the Russian reader is as normal as I am. For a long time now, however, I haven't understood just where the border of Europe runs. Certainly not through the Urals.

I guess you're right.

Well yes. And those who try to draw the European border get very high and mighty and immediately start sounding like politicians. I remember a journalist in Switzerland asking me once whether I considered myself a European. I told him that if he was asking me such a question he did not consider me a European. As soon as someone starts talking about Europeanness a lot of questions occur to me. For example, take some Polish city, or perhaps Vitebsk in Belarus. What makes it more European than Novosibirsk? Nothing. People there study in the same kind of universities and probably as often as not they have an even deeper knowledge of Polish and White Russian literature and art and culture and philosophy — whatever. And they have the same overall — not European but overall — vital interests.

The fact that there is so little specifically Russian in your work makes you unique. Sometimes it isn't even immediately obvious that you are a Russian writer. There are none of those extremes of Russian life that in any case seem to be all around you just now: politics and crime, poverty, wealth, corruption, violence. Do you not see any of this?

I see it in the news. It's part of my life because I'm fearful and alarmed for my family and my life and for my country. I write and talk a great deal about this. I'm interested in what constitutes daily life, however, not in peripheral persons with peripheral professions. Policemen and gangsters, for example, are people of peripheral professions.

But they are visible nonetheless.

Yes, but even policemen and gangsters understand what the norm is. They realize very well that they are living abnormally and that is why they are so careful to conceal or at least not to advertise their private lives which really are horrible and of no interest to anyone. I'm interested in the lives of ordinary people, even wealthy people, especially in Russia. All of them — not just the majority, but all wealthy people of my generation and older without exception — went to the same schools and the same universities and served in the same army. Their wealth came later. We lived identical lives until at least the age of twenty-five. I associate with them a great deal because they are prominent in their fields. I think I have certain interesting merits and they find me interesting. They seek contact with me and I'm interested in them as people who have been very successful. We socialize quite a lot. I have friends and acquaintances among the very rich. We are on an equal footing, which doesn't mean that I ask them for money and they ask me to write a book about them. No, nothing like that ever happens.

Something else about you is unusual. In your works

one doesn't sense any need to get rid of the past, whether Soviet literature or Soviet history.

On the contrary. It's just that I never use the words "Soviet Union" anywhere. Those words are nowhere to be found in any of my works.

Not even in Rivers?

Not even in *Rivers*. There is no mention there of the Komsomol or the Young Pioneers because I assume that my readers are young people who have never been in the Komsomol or the Young Pioneers. They wouldn't understand it, it would alienate them, and they would feel that it isn't about them. This means that when I write about the past and my own past I have to make sure that there is no sense of history that would alienate young readers by leading them to think the book is about other generations and written for adults. I generally try to avoid generational frameworks or features in my books. The fact that my heroes and I don't break with the past, however, comes from my views on life. I clearly understand that I will never again be as happy as I was in childhood, and that I am not going to experience the same joy of life as I did as a child, a joy that had nothing to do with the world order or the political order in Russia, or whatever. I was happy because I was a child, and since I will never be so happy again, my heroes face the time in which they are living rather calmly. They feel and experience very strong emotions and although outwardly they are fairly problem-free, inwardly they are very restless. Describing someone in serious economic straits and how they deal with it is very simple. The hero of *The Shirt*, for example, has his finances in order and he has a job and all the marks of well-being, but he is totally confused and doesn't know how to live.

Yes, and then there is the hero of your play **The City.**

That is precisely what *The City* is about! I saw productions of it in France and Germany, and it is clearly a play that German or French audiences can accept as their own.

That's understandable, but there is one more reason for saying that you are an unusual Russian writer. You mentioned it yourself, namely that you are optimistic, even with respect to Russia.

I know, of course, that practically no generation in Russia has made it to a happy old age surrounded by their children and grandchildren. The world in which every generation has lived has changed radically, thoroughly and harshly, the way it always happens. True, Russians very quickly get used to everything, which is of course also a special quality. I love my Motherland, and I mean "Motherland," and not "this country," which is the usual way to put it. Yes, I say "I love my Motherland."

With a capital "M"?

Yes, a capital "M." I think I know her very well and love her not from Moscow but from outside Moscow. I lived much of my life in Siberia, after all, and that's where I spent my childhood. I spent a long and difficult time in the Navy. Now I live in a completely different place. I travel around the country a lot and I work everywhere. I'm not a tourist here. I know very well how bad it is in the small towns and mining settlements and how poorly our industrial centers are run and how terrible the regional authorities are, and the tyranny... But once again, these are all isolated manifestations. Let's say a policeman stops me and I still don't have my Moscow residence permit. He's rude and theoretically he can arrest me and take me to the station. So that he won't I give him some money, and of course it's all very unpleasant. But it will not make me stop loving my Motherland. Neither will the politicians who regularly torment my country — they won't make me stop loving her either.

Russia very much needs people like you, I think. But as a writer, of course, you observe more than analyze.

Mostly I feel. I have my own explanation for this: I mustn't be observing other people because I'm sure that people do not live in order to be observed. I don't go around challenging life and I don't analyze it. We are not analysts. People who live like my heroes are not analysts or philosophers or psychologists. They are people who feel things keenly and in some way or other are capable of expressing themselves in words. In some way. I insist that what I write is literature based not on observation but on emotional experience. Something else I am sure of is that in the present generation — and with respect to Russian literature I'm a young writer after all, for I began writing just recently — I am one of very few realists. What I write is realistic literature, and that is what very few writers today are capable of. I really mean it: very few are capable. I am a realist writer who maintains the traditions of Russian realist literature. I am totally convinced of this. I say this as a philologist and literary scholar who is capable of evaluating his own work professionally.

I think there is one more trait that allows you to be compared even with Petrushevskaya — you have an awareness of the whole; you capture the collective unconscious and in a way you create a new folklore.

Yes, yes. It's very nice to be compared with Petrushevskaya, especially her early works. She captured her time perfectly; I live in a different time, but of course she's wonderful!

As I've said more than once, I think that you are unique, but the critics say you are working on Chekhov's territory. Which writers do you find congenial?

The writers I find most congenial and love enormously are of course Chekhov and Bunin. Especially *The Life of Arseniev,* which for me may be the most important work in the Russian language. Among earlier authors — Gogol. I know *Dead Souls* almost by heart. And probably Vampilov.[3] Someone has drawn a dotted line between Chekhov-Vampilov and my play *The City.* I won't argue with it. Vampilov was not concerned with being universal. On the contrary, he wrote in great detail and was very much tied to that period. That makes him almost impossible to stage today, but his inborn interest in Chekhov's concept of theater and the way he handles dialogue... Yes, I can say that they're not by any means my teachers but I don't feel alone when I read Chekhov and Vampilov.

You are probably also familiar with foreign authors. Do you find any of them interesting and congenial? Or are they merely interesting and not congenial?

I read Erland Loe's novel *Naïve. Super* with great pleasure. I remember finding out about it from the Internet where someone wrote that there was a novel out by this Norwegian Grishkovets. Yes, that's what they said. I immediately became interested and bought a copy. I liked it a lot and recommended it to many others. It's one of the books I've read recently that made a strong impression on me.

In **Rivers** *you no longer write about the Moscow middle class but turn to your native region. In my opinion*

---

[3] Aleksandr Valentinovich Vampilov (19 August 1937–17 August 1972) well-known playwright in the 1960s and 1970s; born in Siberia.

this is a very powerful and original work. Where did it come from? How did you suddenly begin writing it?

The novel never would have been written if I hadn't left Kemerovo. It's all connected with memories of my grandfather who died in the summer of 1993. As we were leaving I remember my father and me arranging for a tombstone and the grave because we knew we'd very seldom be returning to Kemerovo. So we left and the grave of the man we loved so much remained, and it was so far away... Not long ago — this was a strange adventure — the great Russian director Gleb Panfilov offered me a little role in his film based on Solzhenitsyn's *First Circle*. I played Konstantin Simonov[4] in a very, very brief episode. That was the first time I got dressed up. They put me in a suit made in the Soviet Union. I had never worn a suit made in the Soviet Union because when suits made in the Soviet Union existed I didn't wear suits. And by the time I started wearing sports coats, there were no more Soviet suits. The jacket was brown — you can't imagine the shoulder pads and the cloth, which was only made at Soviet textile factories. So I got dressed and they put on a little makeup and gave me a tie from back then in the forties. I went up to the mirror, and I swear I saw my grandfather — it was as though he'd stepped out of a photograph! We didn't look much alike physically but as I looked at myself I saw a photo — just as though a photograph of my grandfather had come alive. And pow!

---

[4] Konstantin (Kirill) Mikhailovich Simonov (1915-1979) – Soviet writer and public figure, six-time winner of the Stalin Prize, Vice General Secretary of the Soviet Writers Union. In 1958-1960 he lived in Tashkent as a Central Asian correspondent for *Pravda*. In the 1940s he edited the literary journal *Znamya*, and was an editor of *Novyi mir* in the 1950s.

Right then and there came the central, dominant image of my grandfather that I began with. Suddenly it became very important to collect everything, even the little recollections I still had from the stories he told, which are in fact what I reproduce in the book. This seemed very important and valuable because if I were to forget it the man himself would also cease to exist. His grave is far away, thousands of kilometers, but for me he is an important person. Because he is so powerfully present in my life I must somehow preserve all this. That, of course, is not an artistic goal. The artistic goal came along as soon as I began writing.

Your grandfather, of course, is there in **Rivers,** *which contains a lot of autobiographical material on a universal human level. You keep your distance: the name of your hometown isn't even mentioned. You write almost nothing about your family and don't even give the names of your parents.*

Well, you're right. I don't give any names. I don't even mention the names of the rivers.

Why such an approach?

First of all, for the simple reason that Siberia is big and so are the Urals. If I were to mention even the name of a street, people from Tomsk would think that the setting is Tomsk. People from Krasnoyarsk would be sure it's Krasnoyarsk, because there are a lot of coincidences. These cities, by and large, are built the same, and all of them have a river. People from the Urals are absolutely certain that these cities are in the Urals. Not only that, people from Stary Oskol or Kursk tell me that if I hadn't written that the book is set in Siberia they would have thought it was their city.

When I read this work in Finland it seemed like an

attempt to understand Siberia and perhaps through Siberia Russia as well.

It's an attempt to love her because in Russia as soon as you say that you love your Motherland you have to explain a lot about why you love her. Someone with no childhood and no memories can like living in, say, Moscow or Krasnoyarsk or Khabarovsk, but he can't love it. You can like it but loving it is difficult. My story is in fact not even a declaration of love but an attempt to explain why I love it all so much and why it's so difficult to talk about it. Yes, it's a book about how complicated, how difficult it is to talk about loving your Motherland. It's not so important how big or rich the country is. It's probably the same with you there — someone living in, say, Kotka.

An enormous country is something entirely different!

Different, yes, of course…

This is very interesting, and of course for you it marks a new phase.

Absolutely. *Rivers* is a novel with a message, but I feel that everything has changed and that the language in the cycle of short stories I'm working on now is much better. When I had written *Rivers* I realized that the book was older than I am. It is better written than I speak, that is, I don't know how to speak in the way it is written. It's gotten ahead of me.

Yes, it seemed to me that earlier in your plays the language was your own, but in **Rivers** *it's already on another level.*

Yes, it is an entirely different level that I am still trying to get a grasp of by writing a cycle of short stories. In Russian, of course, there are more novels than good short stories.

You have one wonderful story on the Internet — **Pogrebenie angela (Burial of an Angel).**

Yes, yes. *Burial of an Angel* is at present my best work. It is written even more dramatically and powerfully than *Rivers*. There you will also find a complete cycle of three new stories that are thoroughly documentary and based on the life of a young sailor, namely me and my military service. I am also writing one more story about a young man from the provinces. When I finish it the book will be ready and will consist of six stories. That will be it, and from then until April I won't be writing anything but will just work on putting the book together. It will be called *Sbornik proshlogo goda* (*Last Year's Collection*).[5]

Over the past few years you have become, as they say here, a cult figure. You are at present a fashionable "must-read" writer. How does this affect your work? Is it time-consuming?

I've learned to manage my time. I'll put it this way: two or two and a half years ago I wasn't writing books. I didn't have time to write them, and I didn't have any ideas either. As soon as I started to write and develop myself as a writer, literature helped me in many respects to get away from the theater; not get away from, exactly, but to be freer because it helped me discover new territory. I was no longer entirely bound to the theater although audiences were jealous and didn't want to forgive me for leaving the theater and going into literature. But what happened was that as soon as I began getting ideas for books I got the strength — I developed the muscles — to expand my time and channel it into literature. The first time this occurred was when I realized that I had the idea for *The Shirt*. I didn't know then how much time I would need for it, so I took a break for two and a half months. During this period my director Irina was able by extraordinary effort to hold back the torrent of information and other business rushing in from all sides and adjust the work schedule. As a result, I wrote *The Shirt* within just this time frame. I realized that I would need another such period, so I took my next time-out last year to write *Rivers*. Three months this time, over the three months of the summer.

How quickly you write!

Yes, I write very fast. But before actually writing I think a long time. I don't keep any journals. Actually, I'm constantly working and thinking. Then I sit down and write almost without revising.

Does writing give you pleasure?

Not pleasure — happiness, true happiness! I can only write at home, only in Kaliningrad, only under ideal conditions. And this is happiness — to be at home, writing, in this little city, in the winter, and to organize the day as I want, around my writing, to take a walk, and so on. These are happy times. Because of this, of course, my unfulfilled commitments to the theater pile up, so the remaining three months after I finish a book I'm doing plays and traveling almost daily. Just now, December 18, I'm finishing a tour and then no one will see me on stage until March 18. I'll be at home finishing a book.

Your evolution has been remarkable: first — plays; then — short stories; then — a novel; now — **Rivers.** *According to the critic Leonid Kostyukov, these are all merely fragments of an enormous unfinished artistic endeavor. How do you see it?*

I agree, but I can add that this is characteristic of any author who isn't a complete savage and understands what literature or the theater is all about or is interested and involved in the material itself. What is the theater? I'm involved in the phenomenon of the theater, and one way of being involved is to create one play after another as a kind of mega-play. That's what I do. I am writing a mega-play, and similarly all great actors across the world — Russians, Swedes, Americans, whatever, there aren't many of them — have been playing a mega-role. Great writers have been writing a mega-text. I'm not one of them. Instead I'm a kind of cultural figure involved in many different things, the theater, even music. We're doing an album with the group Bigudi, for example, so I'm into a kind of club culture as well, and I'm also writing literature. I'm creating a single cultural image with my hero, who is almost exactly like me. The most important question in contemporary drama, after all, is who is the hero of the play? Who is he? European "social" plays — there are a lot of them — do not answer this question because they produce documentary fragments of life, generally from the social periphery, and they do not address any artistic problems. The heroes of their plays about drug addicts or sexual minorities or the lower classes in London or Berlin will never go to see them. Such heroes do not go to the theater so they and their prototypes never meet.

In your plays it's the other way round!

In mine, yes. It happens in mine. Why do you have to ask who the hero of the play is? Because only when you've answered that question does it become clear how he speaks and what about. I don't know who can be the hero of a play, which is why I said that I am the hero. I know how I speak and I know very well what worries me and what I have gone through. That is what I'm doing. True, I think that I work with the human norm. I have a good sense of it as something pivotal that people can hold on to when they are extremely confused or can't understand their life or are going through a terrible crisis, they can hold on to values of some kind, what has come from the family, the home, their parents, from their favorite films and books. Something to hold on to. At such moments you can also hold on to good food and good weather to help you keep on living. In the final analysis, to honestly earned money as well, something my heroes also take seriously because they work and earn money. They would like to make more, but they can't.

What do you think your life would have been like if you had stayed in Siberia?

I don't think, I know what would have been. I'd be living in Kemerovo, where I had everything as good as the hero of *The City*. If I hadn't left I would have returned to just such a life. Because it was all set. All provincial cities consist of already established routines and familiar people. It isn't much but essentially it can be enough. I would have gotten back into it. And we wouldn't be having this conversation. Or... I would have died. I don't know.

Eduard LIMONOV

*"These are reports from a hot spot —
from my life."*

Eduard Veniaminovich Limonov (Savenko) was born on 22 February 1943 in the town of Dzerzhinsk, Gorky (now Nizhny Novgorod) Region, the son of a soldier. He studied at the Pedagogical Institute in Kharkov (Ukraine). He began writing poetry in 1958. In January 1958 he robbed a store and was then involved in criminal activities until the age of twenty-one. He also worked in a steel foundry and as a steeplejack.

In 1965 he began associating with the literary bohemia in Kharkov. In 1967 he moved to Moscow where he became acquainted with the literary underground joining the unofficial literary and artistic group Concrete (Konkret) in 1971 and attending Arseny Tarkovsky's seminars. For several years he made a living by sewing pants.

Limonov's first collection *Kropotkin and Other Poems* (*Kropotkin i drugie stikhotvoreniya*) appeared in samizdat in 1968, the first of five such samizdat poetry collections.

In 1974 he emigrated to New York, where he worked in 1975-76 as a proofreader for the Russian-language newspaper *Novoe russkoe slovo* and changed jobs 13 times in the space of a few years. Also in 1975-76 he began attending meetings of the Trotskyist Socialist Workers Party.

In 1979 Limonov published his first sensational novel *It's Me, Eddie* (*Eto ya — Edichka*) and the poetry collection *Things Russian* (*Russkoe*).

In the early 1980s he moved to France becoming a French citizen in 1987. In October 1991 he regained his Soviet citizenship and returned to Russia in 1992. In 1990-93 he was a regular contributor to the newspaper *Sovetskaya Rossiya*.

As a journalist he visited Yugoslavia, Abkhazia (Georgia), and the Pridnestrovye region (Moldavia) during the times of civil unrest there. He admits that in all these regions he voluntarily took part in fighting including on three occasions on the side of the Serbs.

In May 1993 he became the leader of the National Bolshevik Front (NBF), shortly thereafter renamed his group of supporters the National Bolshevik Party (NBP) and founded the party newspaper *Limonka* (now banned). In 1993 and 1995 he ran unsuccessfully for the Duma of the Russian Federation.

In April 2001 he was accused of illegal weapon possession, sent to the pre-trial prison of Lefortovo and subsequently spent over two years in prison. This proved to be a very productive time when Limonov wrote a number of books, some dealing with his own experiences, e.g. *Prisoner of the Walking Dead* (*V plenu u mertvetsov*), as well as essays on more general topics such as *The Book of Water* (*Kniga Vody*). In recent years Limonov has continued his oppositional activities, publishing with his own imprint *We Don't Need Such a President: Limonov versus Putin* (*Takoy president nam ne nuzhen: Limonov protiv Putina*), and participating in protest marches during the spring of 2007.

I'd like to talk with you about literature and nothing but literature, about your prose, but in the course of the past few years you have often said that literature means nothing to you, or at least not very much.

Yes, that's what I think. Since 1993 I've been mainly involved in politics. During my prison term — from 2001 through 2003 — unexpectedly for myself I wrote eight books. It's possible that if I had not landed in prison I wouldn't have written anything.

Yet you said recently that since 1980 you've been making your living from literature, and that you have set yourself the goal of living exclusively on that income.

That's correct. I earn money from either literature or journalism. I write for several glossies in Russia and for some online periodicals.

But you're not interested in it?

I'm not. The books I wrote in prison were essays and memoirs rather than fiction. I haven't written a single novel since 1990.

You are praised for your vivid language and perceptive view of the world. Do you always, as it seems, write about yourself or about what you immediately experience and see?

I don't like the novel, and as a consequence my books are not fiction. To some degree they are all essays. Since 1990 I've been writing exclusively in this genre — essays and memoirs.

Is there any period or events in your life about which you have not written?

I'm sure there are events about which I haven't written. The point isn't that, however, but that as in *Memoir of a*

Russian Punk (*Podrostok Savenko*) I've used the pretext of writing through myself and the life of a young man to describe the age. It's set in 1958. Before that there was *The Great Epoch* (*U nas byla velikaya epokha*), set in 1947. That's also supposedly my story, but the period and the people of that period are shown through the story of a child, an adolescent, a youth. It's a kind of news report from the past.

It would be interesting to know how you write in order to create an impression of immediacy. Rapidly, I imagine, and without editing.

I write rapidly, probably everyone does. My reminiscences *The Book of Water* I wrote in 24 days. I write my articles all at once — I just sit down and write and never rewrite.

And you write longhand?

Yes, longhand. After prison I've mainly been writing longhand.

***It seems that you read a great deal while still very young — not only the usual children's books, but Darwin and the* Great Soviet Encyclopedia.**

In one of my books I mention that I used to go to the library. Until I was 15 I didn't like poetry and didn't read any. But a librarian suggested I read Blok, so I read his poems and started writing poetry myself.

So poetry was what you came to like in literature?

Well, I started writing poetry — no matter what I liked or didn't like. I understood that this was a way I could express myself.

But it was as a poet that you began early on, and judging by your trilogy on your youth the fact that you wrote poetry in your younger days had an impact on your life. If

it weren't for that, you probably would have remained in Kharkov, wouldn't you?

I don't know. I don't want to speculate. I don't concern myself with analyzing my life or psychoanalyzing myself. I take myself the way I am.

Your Kharkov trilogy was written in Paris in the 1980s with, as one critic wrote, Gorkyesque lushness. Do you think that you were helped by the fact that you were living abroad then, in another world?

I don't think so. I read Jean Genet's *The Thief's Journal* and thought that it would be good to write something similar because I went through a similar phase at one time in my life. Genet recalls his youth and how he began as a juvenile. So I tried writing about my own criminal adolescence, which resulted in *Memoir of a Russian Punk*, and then wrote all the other books.

What does Kharkov mean to you today?

Absolutely nothing. I haven't kept up contact with anyone. My mother, who is 85, still lives there.

So you visit occasionally?

No. The Ukrainian authorities have denied me entry into the country. I've tried to go. I haven't been there since 1994, when my father died.

In 1967 you settled in Moscow. There have been many big changes in your life, but this must have been one of the most important, involving leaving your hometown and moving into a "different social class" — the class of "real" writers.

I became a poet already in Kharkov but I went to Moscow because I thought I had to be in the center of the country, in the capital where the best writers are gathered. I didn't have a very clear idea of why I went to Moscow but I made the right decision.

And what sort of a reception did Moscow give you?

None whatever. I didn't have a place to live, or a job, or a residence permit, and yet I lived in Moscow for seven years and then left the country.

But you didn't do so voluntarily?

Circumstances were such that it was better for me to leave.

Was it a difficult decision?

You know, I don't think it was so difficult. I was detained by the KGB during that period; they called me in for questioning and finally told me that if I didn't leave I would go to prison. I preferred to leave.

What was the reason?

It's difficult to sort out the reasons. It was the 1970s. The Soviet Union and the KGB were trying to get rid of what they considered to be antisocial elements, including me.

Another and perhaps no less significant stage was your transition from poetry to prose. As you know critics respect you far more as a poet than as a prosaist.

This is some sort of atavism. I haven't been writing poetry for a very long time and I haven't heard any such opinion.

Pyotr Weil, for example, says that a true poet is what you are.

So who is Pyotr Weil?

An essayist and literary scholar. This is his opinion.

It's a shallow opinion. They don't want to admit that someone who lived at the same time with them in New York has written some splendid books. That's a blow to their egos, so they keep repeating that they like me as a poet. I don't even believe they like me as a poet. Their judgments are guided by their egos. They are not objective.

Your literary career began with **It's Me, Eddie.** *Many consider it your most important work, and in* **Prisoner of the Walking Dead (V plenu u mertvetsov)** *you say so yourself.*

I don't remember that. I couldn't have written it because to me all of my books are the best. My books are all different: different periods, different books.

But how do you regard this book today?

I think it's excellent. Well, contemporaries can never have a clear understanding of a book. They'll figure us out afterwards. In any case, I think there was a need for an explosive, revolutionary book. If you can touch the nerve of the age you've been very successful. After that I wrote several more splendid books, including *Prisoner of the Walking Dead* and *Through the Prisons* (*Po tyurmam*) and my memoir *The Book of Water*, all of them splendid. One way or another, people find certain works congenial to them because they correspond to their personal tastes or personal preferences. That doesn't at all mean that this is objectively so. Objectively, if I had only written *It's Me, Eddie*, it would have been just one segment of a circle but I'm a great writer — not a writer with a single theme; I also have other themes, thousands of them.

More on **It's Me, Eddie.** *Yuri Mamleev writes about you: "His first book in prose was written before my very eyes and was full of fury and suffering. It was born out of the life of New York, out of the suffering he endured there."*

I was never friends with Mamleev. What he writes is his business. People write things for different reasons.

All of the characters in your books — your women, your friends -- all are named by name.

Not true — far from it.

Many are, at any rate. And in your own words, you are sometimes "as hard as a rock" and "shamelessly" write about people who were once close to you. Why?

Whom do you mean, specifically?

Perhaps it's difficult for them to read these things?

I wasn't concerned about that.

There is both innovation and tradition in your books. How do you view yourself in the context of Russian literature?

I'm in fact not interested in that either. I like Gogol — *Taras Bulba*, for example. Some of Konstantin Leontiev;[5] I like Bakunin,[6] although he's not exactly a writer. Some things of Dostoyevsky's — the first third of *Crime and Punishment*.

---

[5] Konstantin Nikolaevich Leontiev (1831-1891) – writer, diplomat, philosopher, theorist of Panslavism, secretly took monastic vows at Optina Monastery and settled in the Trinity-St. Sergius Monastery, where he died.

[6] Mikhail Aleksandrovich Bakunin (1831-1891) – active in the political emigration, theorist and practitioner of revolutionary anarchism, Bakunin is noted for saying "The passion for destruction is at the same time a creative passion." The Austrian authorities handed him over to the Russian government, and he spent three years in the Peter and Paul and Schlusselberg prisons and was then exiled to Siberia. Two documents remain from his imprisonment period — his "Confession" addressed to Tsar Nicholas I in 1851, and a letter of 14 February 1857 to Alexander II, which induced the tsar to release him. After escaping from exile through Eastern Siberia, he became politically active in the 1860s in Italy and Switzerland, setting forth his principles in "The International Secret Society for the Liberation of Mankind" and "Revolutionary Catechism." *The Knouto-German Empire and Social Revolution* (1871) and *Statism and Anarchy* (1873) criticize the Marxist view of the role of the state.

I like Khlebnikov as a poet — he's a superb, brilliant twentieth-century Russian poet.

And among contemporary writers?

Generally speaking, writers today don't meet my standards. None of them interest me.

In **The Book of the Dead (Kniga mertvykh)** *you speak of other writers in rather negative terms. You say that Brodsky, for example, is "an utterly mediocre Leningrad poet."*

Well, at one time I was interested in all that but I've gradually lost my interest in literature as such.

It was rather strange to read the Russian press in the summer of 2002. There were articles about Limonov the prisoner and at the same time praise for your latest book, **The Book of Water.** *The critics, for example, called it "serene and wise." Did such reviews give you any consolation in prison? At the time, I think, you were at Lefortovo.*

Well, in the summer of 2002 I was at the Central Prison in Saratov, and it was interesting to read certain reviews. But there are very few intelligent and talented critics. They are just as rare as brilliant writers. Literary criticism basically amounts either to raving about a commodity or panning a commodity.

In one of the books you wrote in prison you have some interesting things to say about the mass media — specifically television and radio. Did you get newspapers there? You don't say much about the print media.

I never intended to write about all this. I wrote about whatever irritated me at the time. I didn't pay any attention to pop culture, this pop Russian music, and I never even turned on the radio. But in Lefortovo I was forced to listen to all this, so I was forced to express my opinion. Not much happens in prison, so you have to express yourself about such trifles. But yes, I was allowed to have newspapers.

And then, in December 2002 you, a convict, were awarded the prestigious Andrey Bely Prize for this same book, for "a good text, as poetic as it is political"...

Well the Andrey Bely Prize isn't much — one ruble and a bottle of vodka.

But the prestige!

I don't know how prestigious it is. I'd prefer to get the Nobel Prize.

You were in prison more than two years. In **Prisoner of the Walking Dead,** *in Lefortovo, you say: "Each day in prison is a battle for your self." How did your work as a writer help you in this battle?*

It certainly did because I hadn't managed to say what I wanted to say when I was free but was able to do so in prison. What I wrote there, however, was not meant to leave the prison. The main feat was to get it to the outside. I was allowed to write but no one gave me permission to send it out. That was the feat — getting my manuscripts out of the prison. I managed to find a way even though I was searched before every interrogation or a meeting with my lawyer.

The manuscripts that you managed to send out — were they read by the prison authorities?

They looked through chunks of them.

They stayed the way you wrote them, at any rate.

There wasn't any censorship, at any rate. I didn't send them out through official channels but passed them on in secret.

You also write that prison is a rehearsal for death. After reading your trilogy it seems to me that this difficult experience was not entirely negative.

I think it was a positive experience — a necessary experience of asceticism, monasticism — a rehearsal for death. I left prison a much wiser man, and I thank prison for it.

Do you have the feeling that you have lost something?

No, I don't have that feeling. On the contrary, I've found something. For me this was extremely necessary.

If I've understood it correctly, you were treated rather well by your cellmates and even the guards.

Yes, I was treated decently everywhere and the explanation is simple. The authorities were sure of themselves — sure of the charges trumped up by the investigative body of the Federal Security Service, the FSB. The General Prosecutor's Office was certain that these accusations were indisputable and that there was no need at that stage to repress me. They hoped that I would be sentenced to some fifteen years, so they didn't recheck the FSB's information. As a result they relied entirely on the sentence. And the trial was even open. Not only because the judge demanded it, the FSB allowed it to be open shortly before it began. They hoped that it would serve as a good lesson and were not at all worried. They had no need to repress me because I was expected to get fifteen years in prison, which, they hoped, I would never leave alive. So there is no contradiction there. Had they known that I would get four years and be out in two and a half, they would have tried to make my life difficult. As it was, they didn't try…

And also you were well known. The media followed you.

Well, they did, but not to the degree they followed Khodorkovsky. And of course the attitude of various groups toward me was not the same. The intelligentsia, for example, did not care much for my reputation although they themselves were responsible for creating it. So grudgingly... but if I'd spent another few years in prison I would have left an even bigger hero.

Russian literature abounds in prison descriptions. Your trilogy is unique nonetheless. It portrays the situation there today, and the inmates are not political prisoners but all sorts of criminals. Did they ask you directly to write about them?

Yes, that's exactly how it was. I got to know several groups of people in *Through the Prisons* who were sentenced either the same time I was or later. There were a lot of prisoners there — about seven thousand during this period in one Central Saratov prison. I couldn't get to know them all but I did tell about some of them. I considered it my duty.

Did they get and read these books afterward?

Yes. I know that one of the heroes of *Through the Prisons*, a man nicknamed Gypsy, managed to read the book. His reaction was positive, of course, because at least I said something about him. He's serving a life sentence and is rotting out there somewhere.

In your prison trilogy there are many direct portraits of prisoners. They are a powerful social commentary and powerful as literature. Are the heroes the inmates rather than you?

Absolutely. That was the goal of the book — to show their lives.

Did you learn anything new about Russia through these lives in this environment?

I was fifty-eight when I went to prison. I didn't learn anything fundamentally new but I did learn something about the backstage, the back alleys of life in Russia, about this terrible hangman's world that is with us every minute and every second. Right here in Moscow there are over seventy thousand people in prison every day. It is a parallel world about which our society either doesn't want to think or constantly forgets. In my view these people are being punished too harshly and cruelly, as is everyone in Russia. Here you can see the cruelty of the state, the cruelty of the laws, human cruelty.

When you met other prisoners, did you have any prejudices?

I wasn't at all prejudiced. What prejudices could there be?

There are so many prejudices in Moscow against the Chechens!

There we all shared the same terrible, tragic fate. The Chechens' fate was even more tragic than ours, and we looked upon them as brothers. How else should we have looked upon them? They were brothers in suffering. It would be another matter if, say, I were to meet them in combat — that would be a different situation. But in that situation we felt they were brothers, and they also felt they were brothers in suffering. All the more so because I'm sure that as people fighting for the independence of their country they deserve respect.

As an observer of prison life you preserve your laconic style but one also senses compassion and respect for the prisoners.

Absolutely. And I think that I managed to say what I wanted to say.

In 1998 you wrote in the foreword to your Collected Works: *"I was just a passer-by in Russian literature." And after that you published more than ten books.*

Well, you see, I assumed one thing but fate decided otherwise. By a twist of fate I wrote another series of books. Just now, by the way, I've finished another one, a political book that was very difficult to publish.

You mean Limonov versus Putin!

Yes, that's another book I didn't think I was going to write but did. It's a kind of indictment, and it was very difficult getting it published. None of the publishers wanted to have it. Ad Marginem refused it. Because there is a lot at stake — it could ruin a publisher. It was published practically underground.

Published underground, yet it's being sold?

It's for sale in the Falanster bookstore and a few others. It's a serious investigative book with a lot of documentation. As I said, an indictment.

Reactions to your works range from complete rejection to profound respect. You yourself are convinced — and I quote you — "What will survive are my books It's Me, Eddie, Diary of a Loser (Dnevnik neudachnika), The Great Epoch, and above all, my fate." Do you remember saying this?

I don't. I wouldn't be decoding statements if I were you because there are so many of them. It's like quoting Karl Marx or the Bible — you can find things that are directly contradictory. I've written a lot, given a lot of interviews... you can't look at what I've said outside of the context and place that I've said it.

You are known to have followers in politics, and now it seems in literature as well. The Limonka Generation: A Collection of Prose by Young Writers Edited by Eduard Limonov (Pokolenie "Limonki" – sbornik molodezhnoy

prozy pod redaktsiey Eduarda Limonova) *has just come out. In what sense are these young authors your followers?*

I didn't edit anything. Others compiled the book and I just lent it my name.

But are all of these writers your followers? Have you read them?

I glanced through it, yes. But I did not edit the book. That was done by someone else.

Does that mean that you don't consider you have a literary school?

We do have a school. In 1994, I founded the newspaper *Limonka* and was editor-in-chief for five years. It became a vehicle for literature and political culture that fostered a certain number of writers. They published their first works with us, and some — far from all — of them were included in *The Limonka Generation.* A lot of people published in *Limonka*, and twelve years later it turns out that an entire school has emerged.

Many consider that "Limonov's fate is the fate of an artist, not of a politician." I don't suppose you agree?

I absolutely don't agree. I have created a rather successful political party, and now that's quite obvious. People are basically one-dimensional. When I was writing poetry, they said they did not like my poetry. When I began writing prose they said my poetry was good but my prose was bad, and when I became a journalist they asked me: "Why are you meddling with journalism? You were a splendid novelist." When I developed from a political journalist into a politician they also began telling me "You're a brilliant writer but a lousy politician." I've cleared these hurdles each time without glancing back at public opinion because if you look back you stop growing. You have to jump higher or run farther, become as big as you can and ignore people who are trying to stop you from growing. I think I'm a very good politician and a lot of people have acknowledged that the past couple of years.

Does this mean that you don't plan on writing any more books?

I don't have any plans; maybe if there's a need to express myself or say something… There was a need for *Limonov versus Putin*, and so I wrote it. I've never said that I'm not going to write but when I've felt that my interests are part of the political struggle I have said so. That's how it is. I wanted to defend myself somehow, and publishing this book was my moral defense. It levels charges against him for Beslan and the Kursk. At least they're not likely to arrest me again because the connection would be too obvious.

Yuri MAMLEEV

"Describing evil does not mean being immersed in it. Instead, you are cleansed of it."

Yuri Vitalievich Mamleev was born on 11 December 1931 in Moscow. His father, a professor of psychiatry, was a victim of the Stalinist terror. In 1956 he graduated from the Moscow Institute of Forestry. While teaching mathematics at a night school he wrote literary works and studied Hindu philosophy, esoterics, and occultism.

From 1953 through 1973 Mamleev wrote hundreds of short stories, two novels, philosophical essays, and poetry, none of which were published. His texts and tape recordings of his readings were disseminated by samizdat. Beginning in 1958 he led an informal esoteric circle calling itself the Sexual Mystics that met at his apartment in Yuzhinsky Lane in Moscow.

In 1974 Mamleev left the Soviet Union and from 1975 through 1983 he lived in the United States where he taught Russian literature at Cornell University. His first publications were in 1975 in the Russian-language journals *Novy zhurnal* and *Tretya volna*. In 1977 a representative selection of his stories appeared in Mikhail Shemyakin's almanac *Apollon 77*.

After the 1980 publication in the United States of his prose collection *The Sky Above Hell* (*Shatuny*), the title of his short novel, Mamleev was invited to join the International PEN Club. In 1983 he moved to Paris, where he continued to teach Russian language and literature at the Institute of Oriental Languages and Civilizations and at the Center for the Study of Russian Language and Literature in Medon.

While in emigration Mamleev achieved a certain international prominence. His works have been published in the West in Russian, English, French, German, and other languages. Since 1989 he has also been publishing in Russia, where he returned after regaining his citizenship in 1991. He participates in international conferences, lectures at universities, and makes radio and television appearances, but his principal interests are literature and philosophy. He teaches Hindu philosophy at Moscow State University and publishes in the journal *Voprosy filosofii* and the almanac *Unio mistica*. In 1999 he received the Andrey Bely Award and the international Pushkin Prize established by the Alfred Topfer Foundation and the International PEN Club.

You are one of the most talked-up serious writers in Moscow. Your books are published and republished, and you make appearances everywhere. How was it in the 1960s, when you were living in Yuzhinsky Lane?

That was during Soviet times, and naturally, works such as mine could not be published, then although there was nothing in them that was particularly political. The aesthetics of the Soviet Union, however, was so restricted to the single vision of Socialist Realism that any Soviet publisher would have been horrified by my works. Yuzhinsky Lane was at that time one of the centers of so called unofficial culture in Russia. The most diverse people gathered there — political dissidents such as Vladimir Bukovsky, well-known artists like Anatoly Zverev and Aleksandr Kharitonov, and poets such as the outstandingly talented Leonid Gubanov. It was a kind of literary-philosophical circle around which were gathered quite a lot of young people, and this was the circle out of which I came. I would read and we would discuss my short stories. Besides Yuzhinsky Lane we met at several other unofficial culture centers in Moscow. Activities were basically readings and art exhibitions.

How do you in retrospect view your role?

At that time we didn't think a whole lot about the future because it was uncertain and contingent on events, and I saw myself as simply one of the founders of a new uncensored Russian culture. Another aspect of the situation was that since we could not hope to get published there was in fact no censorship, and I mean not only the Soviet censors but the internal censor as well. In other words, ours was a situation of absolute freedom. There was no question of any kind of correctness — we were entirely free in all respects, and it was this complete freedom to express and discuss the most diverse questions and problems that compensated for the despotic roof over our heads. At that time I doubt whether even in the United States they would have dared to publish such things.

You weren't afraid?

We weren't afraid because for one thing we all knew one another very well — it was a very tightly knit circle. Secondly, they didn't publish us or let the artists exhibit but they didn't much keep track of what was going on inside —

they knew that it was unacceptable. That sort of persecution concerned mainly outright political dissidents such as Solzhenitsyn or Bukovsky.

To what extent does your arguably most gloomy and best-known novel **The Sky above Hell** *reflect that period of your life?*

I wrote it just at that time and it was precisely that absence of any sort of censorship, including the internal one, which allowed me to write it. It touches upon the most painful questions of human existence — questions people usually don't want to talk about. It is of course not such a very exact reflection of reality — it is a work of art, not a documentary — but there were prototypes. It reflects reality artistically and, as sometimes happens in literature, intensifies it. By that I mean that all of these problems existed but not in such an explicit and grotesque form as in the novel. That is why it had such resonance — because everything in it was hyperbolized, so to speak, and all the dark sides were illuminated.

I'm quoting: "According to accounts of those who knew Mamleev in the '60s, he differed little from his own heroes. Fear of death, drunkenness, a bohemian lifestyle and his writing itself, which was borderline pathological, shattered his nervous system. He painted his monstrous heroes from life."

That's true, of course, but it's very superficial and partial. The thing is that at that time all of Russia was on a binge. We were no different from anyone else in that respect. Secondly, that comment about my shattered nerves is completely incorrect. When a writer creates a work he is, on the contrary, reinforced spiritually through catharsis, a well-known process in aesthetics. Describing evil does not mean being immersed in it. Instead, you are cleansed of it. So my nerves weren't shattered and neither were anyone else's.

But you yourself said at some point: "This novel was written in the deep underground in Moscow in a desperate situation when it seemed that all hope had collapsed, including my belief in immortality..."

Yes, absolutely correct. That is a precise description of the situation and, of course, a writer never completely resembles his heroes but should always stand above them. If he himself were the hero he could not create them. In my case at any rate there was a certain estrangement: I was in a certain sense dispassionate and sometimes passionate but I was an observer, like a student or researcher. Art was the means by which I came to know the unusual depths of the human soul — Dostoyevsky's approach, basically.

In The Sky Above Hell *the world is Hell and people are monsters. Many of your strange characters are horrible murderers or repulsive self-tormentors who can certainly be approached on various levels, but have you as the author ever felt disgust toward them?*

Yes, and not only disgust and not only with respect to *The Sky Above Hell*, but to other stories as well. As I was emerging from the state I was in when I wrote and returning to my usual everyday condition I was sometimes horrified at what I had written. But I understood that artists have to make certain sacrifices in order to create.

Are you saying that you wrote your texts in some sort of special state?

Absolutely correct. I wasn't — not by any means! — under the influence of drugs or alcohol, because in such a state I don't think I could write anything. No, it was something resembling a meditative state. I am an Indologist, after all; I've taught Hindu philosophy and have always been interested in the East. It was simply a state in which I was able to glimpse such strange, unusual corners of the human soul. It wasn't an everyday state, and so I went in and out of it.

When you wrote did you remain in this state for several hours?

Yes, more or less. At first it was very difficult to enter it but then it became more natural and I could stay in it for two or three hours. I usually did not write more than three hours at a stretch and then I would somehow come out of it.

Why do you have to demonstrate so many different kinds of extremely cruel and macabre evil? Your destructiveness has a philosophical, metaphysical aspect, doesn't it?

Yes, quite correct. But I have to say that my most recent novels — *Erring Time* (*Bluzhdayushchee vremia*), *The World and the Laugh* (*Mir i khokhot*), and *The Other* (*Drugoy*) are different from *The Sky Above Hell*. With respect to the philosophical background or subtext, *Erring Time*, is an answer to the questions that are brought to a head in *The Sky Above Hell*. In it there is light, there is hope, there is faith. As for that destructive period, it was necessary. It was rather like an initiation, where you first must immerse yourself, so to speak, in the reverse image or negative of the world, and only then can you struggle out into hope, light, and lucidity. In the East this is a very common path to the light.

Can **The Sky Above Hell, Erring Time, and The World and the Laugh** *be considered a trilogy?*

Perhaps in a philosophical sense, yes. These novels are completely different because *Erring Time* was written in today's Russia, and *The Sky Above Hell* in the Soviet Union. But it is certainly possible to connect them with a thread, in which case they would resemble a trilogy in which answers to the questions posed in *The Sky Above Hell* gradually emerge. As the American writer James McConkey[7] put it, the humor in *The Sky Above Hell* is deadly but its subtext is metaphysical.

It seems to me that in this grotesque, fantastic world of **The Sky Above Hell** *almost all the characters are asking themselves one single question: what is beyond death?*

Yes, the question is what is beyond death. But as to the philosophical subtext there is another important component, namely the sense that the world is an illusion. As American critics wrote about my protagonist Fyodor Somnov, he kills because he is searching for eternity. He clearly looks upon this world as an illusion and prays for the souls of the people he has murdered.

You have also written one "realistic" novel — **The Moscow Gambit** *(Moskovskii gambit). How factual is it?*

It is thoroughly realistic and to a considerable extent factual but still a literary work. There you find descriptions of Yuzhinsky Lane and other salons in Moscow. The only purely fictional figure is the protagonist Aleksandr Trepetov, who is simply a concentrate of all the spiritual and intellectual quests that were

---

[7] James McConkey – essayist and novelist, Professor Emeritus of English at Cornell University. His work explores the theme of memory. The anthology *The Anatomy of Memory* was published by Oxford University Press in 1996 following upon his autobiographical work *Court of Memory (1983)*.He has written several books of essays, including *To a Distant Island* (2000); *The Telescope in the Parlor: Essays on Life and Literature* (2004), and *Chekhov and Our Age*(1985).

taking place there. Readers have been able to identify some of the prototypes. It's quite obvious who they are.

What was it like growing up in the Soviet Union?

My youth was more or less typical of the Soviet intelligentsia of the time. My father was a psychiatrist and my mother graduated from the Department of Geography at Moscow University. By Soviet standards we lived relatively well in the 1930s, but then my father was arrested on political grounds for "anti-Soviet views", according to the dreaded Article 58 that was used to arrest so many people. During and after the war my mother brought me up alone and of course life was difficult. She had some help from her sister, however, who was a professor and a gynecologist, and her husband, Isaak Solomonovich Zhorov, also a professor, a surgeon, and an anesthesiologist.

Your father was in the camps at the time.

Yes, he died in the camps. So that was our situation.

You said that your father was a psychiatrist and your relatives were also doctors. Has this fact influenced you as a writer in any way?

Yes, you could say that it has because other relatives and close friends of our family were also doctors and psychologists, and through them I learned about many unusual cases that I later described in *The Sky Above Hell* — the boy that made soup out of his own body, for example. I knew psychiatry from my father's books but I was not so very interested in real insanity or obvious illnesses like schizophrenia and manic-depressive psychosis; instead I took an interest in so-called borderline psychopathy on the boundary between health and mental illness because people in such a state are not afraid and do not conceal what ordinary people do.

Are there any works of Soviet literature that still have any significant relevance for you?

It depends on what you mean by the term "Soviet." Take Bulgakov or Platonov, for example, who lived during Soviet times but in essence were Russian writers who grew up in the pre-revolutionary period. Their works are in fact a continuation of the Russian classics. Or the literature of the 1920s — Pilnyak, for instance — all of this is something completely different. Even Aleksey Tolstoy and Gorky were classics of Russian literature. Soviet literature in the real sense began after World War II, when this generation was already gone, and here I don't think anything has touched me at all. Another thing is the appearance of unofficial literature — the poetry of Gubanov and Brodsky, Solzhenitsyn, and — I still like it — Venechka Erofeev's immortal poem *Moscow to the End of the Line*, which the French have called "the Iliad of Russian alcoholism." I knew Erofeev personally, he was close to our Yuzhinsky circle. I read his book in a samizdat edition his closest friend had given me. At the time it made a very touching and profound impression.

How was it that you began writing?

I was always quite obviously inclined to literature and philosophy, and even my teachers noticed it. One was Yevgeny Rudolofovich, a physicist. He was a very erudite man of the old pre-revolutionary generation. Because of his origins he could not teach at Soviet universities despite his extraordinary knowledge of physics, so he taught at our school. A very well educated man! And he gave me this advice: "Yura, whatever you do don't enroll in any institute of the humanities because, first of all, it's easy to get yourself arrested there." The second reason was that literature is always such a sea of the unknown.

"It's better," he said, "to have some practical profession you can make a living at." My relatives also advised me not to take chances by going into the humanities, especially since my father had been arrested. It was all the same to me which technical college to enroll in, so I entered the institute of forestry. That's how it went. When I graduated they gave me an engineering degree. Because the forestry department offered mathematics and physics, I was qualified to teach these subjects at high school.

When you were living in Yuzhinsky Lane and teaching mathematics were you harassed?

We were all under surveillance, of course. They kept an unofficial file on all writers and artists involved with unofficial culture. They would even conduct surveys, asking people who had seen or read our works about us. Some of those people later told me they were constantly asking about me: what I was like, about my works, etc. But they never summoned me because, as one of my women readers told me, they said: "We simply can't understand what sort of person he is and why he writes such things. There isn't anything particularly political in them. We call in people when there is something specific, when we know who he is and what we can charge him with." So that was their reaction.

Why did you decide to emigrate in 1974? And why did they let you?

They let me for the simple reason that at the time there was a secret regulation to let out so-called dissidents together with the Jews. It was a small trickle and as dissidents they classified not only political figures such as Solzhenitsyn, Maksimov, and Sinyavsky, but also non-conformist writers and artists on whom they had files and who were known in unofficial art circles. On this basis it was possible to leave. If some outsider they didn't know were to come along he would only run into problems. But — take note! — artists such as Shemyakin and my friends Tselkov and Oskar Rabin also emigrated. They were simply artists, not at all politically active — what did they have to do with politics! — but on the basis of this dissident regulation non-conformist artists got out. It was not only possible to leave but desirable.

So it was a simple process. But the decision must have been difficult?

Yes, the process itself was simple because they were trying to get rid of us, but of course it was a difficult decision. At first we thought of living in the Soviet Union and publishing in the West but then along came a law that criminalized any transfer of unofficial manuscripts to the West without the knowledge of the official writers' organizations. This law was not enforced very often, but when it appeared that was it — my wife and I decided that writers should at least be published in their lifetime. For that reason quite a few writers and artists left the Soviet Union at that time.

The critics even seem to be afraid of your works. Instead of entering this nightmarish world they pin all sorts of labels on you: black absurdist, conceptualist, surrealist... Now you call yourself a metaphysical realist. Is this a new literary trend in Russia?

Yes, entirely new. I give a philosophical substantiation of it in "The Metaphysics of Art" (Metafizika iskusstva), the concluding chapter of my book *The Fate of Being* (*Sud'ba bytiia*). The essence of it is that realistic narration is supplemented with elements of metaphysics in the broad sense — that is, everything beyond the boundaries, as it were, of the visible world. It depends on the writer's intuition, familiarity with the spiritual traditions, and personal convictions or worldview. It excludes fantasy, however, because the whole thing is that it derives from the knowledge, which humanity has collected about this sphere on the other side of life, and it is based on the writer's intuition. The principle of metaphysical realism is that the action takes place on both sides — here and there, as it were. Not in the literal sense "there" but from there, at least, should come some sorts of visions, rays, etc.

One critic writes: "I think that the phenomenon that is Mamleev will bother literary scholars for many years to come. Obviously, no one dares to take on such unfathomable material." Do you find any of the critical reactions to your works interesting or do you usually feel that the critics don't understand you?

No, no. They understand very well, although perhaps not entirely. As you yourself have said, there are many levels in my works. Now, however, dissertations and monographs are being written about me in Russia, and from what I've heard, they are doing graduation theses in the West. A young woman at the University of Venice sent me a remarkable graduation thesis, and there was one from Germany. The criticism overall in the newspapers varies: some of it is impressionistic, some tries to go deeper. There is a lot of it now, I have whole folders of articles in French, German, English, Italian, and Russian — none of them on a scholarly level, however. This criticism is impressionistic, and sometimes it is based less on my works than on interviews with me in which I attempt to explain my works. On some level they do become intelligible. I have lots of young readers who are — I'm not afraid to use the word — my fans. They like my works, and some very strange things are happening. Not long ago, in the 1990s, two Russian musicians in Berlin wanted to commit suicide. They just happened to come upon *The Sky Above Hell*, and they took turns reading it all night. It made such an impression on them that they said: "We are not going to commit suicide because life is so fantastic and interesting that we want to live!" In other words, my novel had the opposite effect — catharsis. I've heard that this is what happens in many cases. Some people, of course, are put off. "I can't read this," they say. "It will destroy me." Others say, "Yes, it's gloomy but because of the way it's done the power of art is beneficial." A third group, like these musicians, say "No, deep down there is something that makes you want to live!" Indeed, love of life is very strong in this novel. Why do people search for immortality? Because they want to live forever. Because what is in the book is not what destroys life. It is desperation but at the same time it's a kind of quest for eternal life. It is based on the desire to live, the desire to be immortal.

Your novels and stories are often set in strange, neglected little places on the outskirts of Moscow among public toilets and scrap heaps — quite a marginal milieu. I don't suppose there are any such places in the Moscow region any more.

These places were in the Soviet Union. In my latest novel *The Other* there is a New Russian who lives in a luxurious house. He is my hero living not in a marginal milieu but, on the contrary, in wealthy circumstances. That is the first point. The second is that in *Erring Time* and *The World and the Laugh* what I stress is not the rundown condition of these little houses but rather their isolation. Some of them are quite decent but they are isolated, and such little nooks still exist.

In some places you can still see a lonely little house on the edge of a cottage area, for example, near a dump.

These are strange, surrealistic surroundings, like something out of a dream.

Yes, it is a somewhat strange environment. German soldiers who came to Russia in World War II write in memoirs that everything in the Soviet Union struck them as a dream, a surreal landscape. Much of what from a general point of view seems surreal is reality in Russia.

In The Sky Above Hell *and in certain stories there are important encounters between simple folk and representatives of the intelligentsia.*

Yes, they do occur, and such encounters are still taking place. In *The Other*, there is one such meeting. Sometimes now as well, in bars or other places, marginal elements and the intelligentsia intersect. There are some very interesting encounters with such people, by which I don't mean criminals or thugs in the literal sense but people somewhere on the border. Why do they interest intellectuals and why are they interested in art? It's because intellectuals themselves often live in a borderline state. Or sometimes these simple people are quite extraordinary — in Russia there is no such social differentiation — you can find spiritually superior individuals at the very bottom of society. Once I happened to get into a conversation with a simple young man — a soldier who had been in a lot of hot spots — an ordinary simple person. "How did you manage to survive there?" I asked. He answered: "I read Platonov." Amazing!

It seems you have been writing stories all your life — there must be hundreds of them. Where do you get your themes?

Sometimes something suggests a subject to me — not the newspapers, however. Dostoyevsky, as you know, sometimes took his plots from the newspapers. It can be just an anecdote someone told me in a casual meeting.

And then something gets going?

It just gives me a push. Take the story "Macroworld" (Macromir), for example, in which a young man jumps from the fifth floor on a bet. How was this plot born? At the time I was teaching at a school for working-class youth (which is what they called schools for adults who dropped out of secondary school to begin working). One day I came into the classroom and noticing that one student was absent I asked about the reason. They told me what had happened. He had been drinking vodka with someone and on a bet he put on his coat and jumped out the window to his death. I was of course dumbfounded, as were his classmates. I thought that maybe he was insane, yet he didn't impress me that way. So on the basis of this incident, for which there may have been some kind of explanation, I wrote "Macroworld." I reworked it into a story without really changing anything but I added a psychological, psychopathological and metaphysical subtext.

I think that it is the stories that show interesting changes in your writing. The young Mamleev is often amusing and impetuous but the mature Mamleev is serious and more depressing. How do you see this evolution?

That is how it should be. I started with tales of everyday life. The German edition of my works includes many of these early stories because they are funny, humorous. Later, as I got involved with serious things such as philosophy and global problems, they became very different. In my latest works, however, especially those that went into *The Other*, there is more catharsis, there is enlightenment — in many instances, even though the story itself is horrible, you can see light. The cycle of stories in this new book, for example, begins with *Evening Meditations (Vechernie dumy).* The plot is taken from real life. Somebody told me this story. A real killer, a burglar, entered an apartment thinking that the owners were away. But he was wrong. There were two adults at home, a man and a woman in their forties, evidently weak persons. He killed them both. Someone must have thought that they had something worth stealing — gold, money. No matter, he killed them. But then out of another room came a little boy of five or so. And it was around Easter. He came out and said to the burglar: "Christ is risen." It was so eerie that the man fainted. What happened to him then I don't know. I suppose he was arrested. But I continued the story by letting the killer get away and at the end of the story he meets the boy who said to him "Christ is risen."

What was it like to return home from emigration?

We also live in France. When Gorbachev and then Yeltsin came to power, they apologized to many non-conformists and told us that we could live wherever we wanted — in France, Germany, America, but also in Russia. Returning was a stunning experience, of course, because except for a few people, like Gubanov, almost all those I associated with, including my relatives, were still alive. When after fifteen years you see your friends, admirers, relatives, with whom you spent the whole time before that, it is of course a shock on the personal level. My wife was also shaken because her mother was living here. All in all, these new meetings were fine but on the social level we realized that Russia was already a different country. Everything was seething, there were demonstrations, meetings, and so on. To a significant degree, in fact, the intelligentsia had become more or less the same as the unofficial stratum in the 1960s. At that time the mainstream intelligentsia was very Soviet and served the Soviet regime — everyone. Even Pasternak wrote about Stalin, and it was the same with Aleksey Tolstoy and the official Soviet writers. And suddenly we saw that intellectuals rejected Communism just like that thin stratum back in the 60s. It was an entirely different situation.

Today you are a cult writer and the leader of the school of metaphysical realism you mentioned. There is even a "Metaphysical Realism Club" at the Central Writers' House.

The writer Sergey Sibirtsev organized all that. Members of the club include well-known writers such as Anatoly Kim, Vladimir Makanin, and others. One of the new writers, Olga Slavnikova said: "If there is anything at all that extends realistic narration we want to connect to it and develop it." That is, not as I do in my works but at least somewhat in the same direction because it can't be done all at once. And they want to join together under my banner. The main thing, however, is that they are young, and they express the metaphysical element to a much higher degree and more directly. AST Publishers has put out a collection of young writers of the metaphysical school, and other collections are in the works. My readers and admirers are basically young people.

But you also have a literary heir who is a little older. I mean Vladimir Sorokin.

Vladmir Sorokin is somewhat off by himself: he does not yet belong to our movement. He says he considers himself my pupil but he is very independent. His works are in a category all their own.

In 1991 you regained your Russian citizenship. In 2000 you were awarded the prestigious Pushkin Prize. What is it like to live and work in Russia now?

My work is going well but writing always involves a certain tension. We spend a lot of time in Europe, in France and Germany. I think that our age is an age of unification or a kind of coming together, but like all transitional periods it is rather dramatic.

Victor PELEVIN

"Reality is any hallucination you believe in one hundred per cent."

Victor Olegovich Pelevin was born on 22 November 1962 in Moscow. His father taught military science at the Bauman Engineering Institute, and his mother was a schoolteacher. Having finished school in 1979, he entered the Moscow Power Engineering Institute, graduating in 1985. In 1987 he went on to postgraduate school there until 1989. In 1988 he enrolled in the correspondence department of the Literary Institute, where he attended the seminar of the Russophile Mikhail Lobanov. In 1991 he was expelled.

Pelevin has been contributing short stories to various newspapers and journals since 1989. For several years he worked for the journal *Nauka i religiya* (*Science and Religion*), where he edited materials on Oriental mysticism and in 1989 published his first literary work, the fairy-tale "Sorcerer Ignat and People" ("Koldun Ignat i lyudi"). In 1990 he became the editor of the prose section of the newly founded Den publishing house.

Pelevin is the author of several novels: *Generation P* (1999), *Numbers* (*Chisla*), which is included in *The Dialectics of the*

Transitional Period From Nowhere to Nowhere: Selected works (*Dialektika Perekhodnogo Perioda iz Niotkuda v Nikuda: Izbrannye proizvedeniya*; 2003), *The Sacred Book of the Werewolf* (*Svyashchennaya kniga oborotnya*; 2004), and *Empire V* (2006). *The Helmet of Horror: The Myth of Theseus and the Minotaur* (*Shlem uzhasa: kreatiff o Tesee i Minotavre*; 2005) is part of the international Canongate "World Myths" series.

The 1993 laureate of the Little Booker Prize, Pelevin was also awarded the Richard Schönfeld Prize for satire in Germany in 2000 and the National Bestseller Prize and Apollon Grigoriev Award in 2003. His books have been translated into all the major languages, including Japanese and Chinese.

You and I have met once already, in 1997 at the Lukomorye Café. At that time you described Russians as deep-water fish. When they finally swim up to the surface and see the sun their internal pressure becomes too great and they explode. What is the situation like eight years later?

I'm full of optimism. The thing is that it turned out the sun wasn't real, so nothing is threatening the fish.

Back then in 1997 you were still talking about how literature programs life. You had just had some experience of that because after your story about a certain cruel mayor was published in the **Ogonyok** *weekly, almost the same thing happened in "real life." Then it seems that before September 2001 you wrote a text in which the demiurge hero destroys two twin towers.*

That was a fleeting theme in an unfinished novel, and I'm glad that it remained unfinished. I think that the world just then was pregnant with this ghastly event, which was simply bursting through the cracks. The future approaches the present like the airplane toward the tower. No one can see anything yet, it's unclear what will happen, but there's already a shadow reflected in the windows. Such things happen. Blok's poetry at the beginning of the century, for example, was already pregnant with the revolution.

Let's talk about a different kind of programming. You grew up in Moscow in the 60s and 70s. What made the strongest cultural impression on you in your childhood? What books did you read at home?

Everything on the shelf. But there weren't any cultural impressions back then — only existential ones.

Is there anything in Soviet culture that you find especially congenial and interesting? Any works that you still consider relevant?

Any text that I'm reading at a given moment is relevant. This is the only thing that makes it relevant. As soon as I stop reading it, it loses its relevance.

You chose — and graduated from — the Moscow Power Engineering Institute. Why?

I didn't choose — I was 16 when I enrolled there. It was my parents' choice. I didn't have any personal plans for my life, so I disliked equally all of the careers that were possible in the USSR.

Your father was in the military, serving in the Air Force. You yourself served there. How did that experience affect your writing?

My father served in an anti-aircraft defense unit — the PVO in Russian — so that's why my initials are PVO — Pelevin, Victor Olegovich. I've loved airplanes since I was a child and was constantly drawing them in my school notebooks. But I never served in the Air Force. My military occupational specialty was the electrical system of the MIG fighters, which I studied at the Institute.

Why did you decide to become a writer? How did you start out?

I wrote a short story that just came into my head. It gave me enormous pleasure, so I went on trying to experience this sensation again and again. It resembles a sexual experience.

Nabokov comes to mind when I read your works. I know that Platonov and Bulgakov are also congenial. When and how did you first read them?

As a child. Somebody gave me a samizdat copy of Platonov's *The Foundation Pit* to read overnight. I had to read fast, so it was a complex experience. Bulgakov I read in the journal *Moskva* at the Nekrasov Public Library. Nabokov showed up later when I was in the tenth grade.

You've been publishing stories since 1989, but **Omon Ra** *can be considered the beginning of your career. You wrote that novel during the year the Soviet Union was disintegrating. Do you today see any of the events then reflected in the novel?*

Omon Ra is the last novel written in the USSR — I finished it the day before the 1991 putsch that doomed the country. To me that seems symbolic. In effect the novel explains why the USSR fell apart.

You were subsequently obliged to repeat many times that **Omon Ra** *is about the inner space or cosmos of the Soviet individual, not at all about the space program.*

Outer space is a projection of the inner cosmos. We and the Americans flew to different spaces. Note that Soviet space explorers are called "cosmonauts" in English, whereas American cosmonauts are "astronauts." Check the Oxford dictionary.

Have you ever wondered what would have happened to you if the Soviet Union had not collapsed?

I'd have probably collapsed myself.

The transformation of the Soviet Union into Russia is of course an important theme of yours. It seems to me that sometimes it has to do with nostalgia — in Generation P, *for example, when Tatarsky remembers the thrill of his first pair of new sneakers ten years ago...*

It's not nostalgia for the social system but nostalgia for your youth. People often think that they are longing for the old days but in fact they are longing for themselves when they were young.

Now an unavoidable question: Generation P *— what does that stand for? For me the letter "P" is also connected with the word "pleasure." In that novel your linguistic inventiveness wonderfully illustrates dubious social changes.*

"P" stands for the entire cluster of graphic Russian words beginning with this letter. You know what I mean.

At the same time the book is very funny. It must have been both fun and misery to write.

Indeed it was.

In Generation P *everyone is searching for the national idea. Today, in Putin, have they found it?*

Of course. That's precisely what Putin is.

After Generation P *you fell silent as a writer for four years. What is your own retrospective view of what happened? Was there some sort of sudden change in your writing?*

I wasn't silent but I simply didn't publish anything during that time. Moreover, a writer needs periods of silence.

Your next book — **The Dialectics of a Transition from Nowhere to Nowhere** *is the "Pelevin of today," meaning a more abstract and intellectual narrative. In it is a story entitled "A Macedonian Critique of French Thought" (Makedonskaya kritika frantsuzskoy mysli.) Why were you so interested in writing so much about Baudrillard and Derrida, for example?*

I was interested in making these intellectuals the heroes of a pointedly unintellectual text. It's like appointing Schwartzenegger a governor, only the other way around.

I think that the difference between the " young" Pelevin and "today's" Pelevin is clear if one compares **The Sacred Book of the Werewolf** *with the earlier story "The Problem of the Werewolf in Central Russia" (Problema vervolka v Sredney polose). What is your view of the "young" Pelevin?*

If you think about it, it's like the haze over a wave
Between me and you, between the shallows and
the drowning;
Or I see telephone poles and you from the back
As you pedal your half-racer straight into the sunset.[8]

I must admit that my favorite book of yours is still the witty, poetic, and melancholy **The Life of Insects (Zhizn nasekomykh).** *What is yours?*

Mine is *The Sacred Book of the Werewolf.* It has a lot of personal associations for me.

---

[8] A quotation from Vladimir Nabokov's poem "You and I Had Such Faith" ("My s toboyu tak verili"). (My translation; *CR*.)

You've been criticized rather often for your female characters (which, incidentally, seem entirely normal to me in **The Life of Insects***). Is that perhaps why you wanted* **The Sacred Book of the Werewolf** *to have a female narrator?*

No, it was the heroine who wanted the book to be written in the first person.

There have been other criticisms. In **The Dialectics of a Transition from Nowhere to Nowhere** *and* **The Sacred Book of the Werewolf** *many already familiar things are repeated. But that cannot be said about your novel* **The Helmet of Horror***. Does it represent a new approach?*

You know, all people repeat themselves when they wake up in the morning. In addition, all my books contain the very same letters of the alphabet. There is something to be said about that as well. I don't know what a new approach or old approach is. The reader is looking for something other than novelty in a book. Nor does a writer write a book to say something new. For him it's the same sort of act as making a web is for a spider. If a fly comes along and says "there's nothing new in this web," the spider can be sure that it has accomplished its task.

Do you have a clearly thought-out plan when you begin writing a story or novel? How, for example, did you begin **The Helmet of Horror***?*

In horror.

Let's talk a little about that novel. You are probably a pioneer among Russian writers in using the Internet, and if I'm not mistaken, the Internet for you is a kind of space of freedom. In **The Helmet of Horror***, however, the Internet becomes a labyrinth, even a prison.*

The Internet is not a space of freedom. Only the mind can be a space of freedom. Everything into which the mind is put becomes its prison.

The Helmet of Horror *combines elements of Buddhist philosophy and Internet chat rooms. How are the Internet and Buddhism connected?*

In my mind.

When and how did you become acquainted with Buddhism?

It was about two thousand years ago in Benares. I don't remember the exact circumstances.

To me, Buddhism in your works is a space and unexpected possibilities, as in the story "The Life and Adventures of Shed Number XII" (Zhizn i priklyucheniya saraya Nomer XII").

Buddhism is a label that can be pasted on my books. I don't mind. You don't have to paste it. I don't mind that either. Buddhism is simply consciousness of the fact that everything takes place only in the mind.

Why are you so interested in psychodelic experiences?

I'm no longer interested. Sobriety is stronger than drugs.

What is your favorite science fiction novel?

Andromeda. A Space-Age Tale (*Tumannost Andromedy*) by Ivan Yefremov.

What do you think of the film **The Matrix?**

The first one was good. The rest are an ordinary commercial product but not very effective.

Today you are one of the most famous writers in Russia. How adequately have your works been received there?

I don't know. I don't even know how adequately I'm writing them.

You have often said that there is nothing worse for a writer than to participate in this so-called literary life. Yet you react rather strongly to criticism. In **Generation P,** *for example, you put the critic Pavel Basinsky in the outhouse...*

President Putin has called upon us to waste our enemies in the crapper. Nothing personal.

You say that you simply write for others the kind of books you yourself would find entertaining. Is that perhaps why in your early works there is often a happy ending or at least a way out?

There is no way out. And that is the way out.

In the case of **The Helmet of Horror** *it is impossible to speak of a happy ending. On the contrary, some think that this novel marks the end of Russian postmodernism. Do you perhaps see any way out of this labyrinth?*

Stop thinking that you are in a labyrinth.

Ludmila PETRUSHEVSKAYA

Giovanna del Magro

"Soviet literature made me into a fiery, honest, principled and implacable enemy of this literature and this order."

Ludmila Stefanovna Petrushevskaya was born on 26 May 1938, the daughter of a Moscow University professor. She graduated from the Department of Journalism at Moscow University in 1961. In 1972 she worked as an editor at the Central Television Studio. She began writing stories in the mid-1960s, publishing the first two in the journal *Avrora* in 1972. From the mid-1970s she also began writing plays. In 1977 her *Music Lessons* (*Uroki muzyki*) was staged by Roman Viktyuk. In 1979 her one-act play *Love* (*Lyubov*; 1974) was published in the journal *Teatr* and was included in the 1981-82 repertoire of the Taganka Theater. In 1983 *Music Lessons* and *A Glass of Water* (*Stakan vody*) were playing on Moscow stages, and *Three Girls in Blue* (*Tri devushki v golubom*) was put on by the Lenkom Theater. Universal recognition came in 1985 with a play based on her *Columbine's Apartment* (*Kvartira Kolombiny*) at the Sovremennik Theater.

Petrushevskaya's first prose collection *Immortal Love* (*Bessmertnaya lyubov*) did not appear until 1987. In 1991 she was awarded the German Pushkin Prize. Her novel *The Time Night* was short-listed for the first-year Russian Booker Prize. She is the author of many stories, novellas, and plays, as well as animated film scripts. A five-volume collection of her works was published in 1996 by AST publishers in Moscow and Folio in Kharkov. In 2004 her novel *Number One, or in the Gardens of Other Possibilities* (*Nomer Odin, ili v sadakh drugikh vozmozhnostey*) appeared with Eksmo.

THE MAKING OF A SOVIET WRITER
(An Attempt at a Confession)

How does one become a writer? Essentially, of all the creative professions, this one is the simplest to get into. All you have to know is how to read and write — that is, you must complete at least the first two grades of elementary school (whereas musicians, artists, and actors must have special training).

During the Soviet period, anyone who wanted to become a writer (or more precisely, a member of the Soviet Writers' Union) could do so. All that was required was to be able to set forth your thoughts coherently and to observe certain ideological rules.

True, usually this was preceded by a love of reading and a compulsive propensity for scribbling. Yielding to this inclination, the future writer generally first had to pass through an initial stage — that is, he or she would usually begin writing rather idiotic poetry — and not until everyone grew tired of hearing it would the unsuccessful poet switch to prose. (A poet can be considered a poet when outsiders — not Mom and Dad but distant acquaintances and strangers — offer praise and are prepared to listen. That is, when the poet has acquired some readers.)

But it can be even simpler! All you need to become a writer is to get published. That is, you have to find someone who is willing to take a chance and print your prose. True, we all know how long we can wait for such an event. Kafka, for example, didn't live to see it. In Soviet times, however, future writers had a fairly simple course of action: write a novel about a factory, or construction, or the work life of young people, and make sure to include a kindly and wise Party activist. As the Soviet poet Tvardovsky said on this subject, the plot in a *kolkhoz* novel should be simple: "A retrograde vice chairman, a progressive chairman, and a grandpa looking forward to Communism." Works like that could be sent to the publishers, and with a little pushing they would be published. Two published novels and you're a member of the Writers' Union, which lets you go on business junkets — even abroad — at state expense, and stay at seaside retreats, and you can expect a free apartment, a car, furniture and a refrigerator (not free but no waiting in line), and a dacha at Peredelkino. I should explain that in order to get an apartment, a car, or a summer cottage, not to mention a refrigerator, ordinary Soviet citizens filled in applications, were entered on waiting lists, and waited for years for their turn at their work place. If they changed jobs they lost their place in line and had to start all over again. So there you have the advantage of belonging to the Writers' Union, where all these good things were distributed far more generously! A lot of people wanted to be accepted.

As for writers who wrote about the hardships of life and love under Soviet conditions, they never became members of the Writers' Union. In other words, what engendered new writers were correct themes and ideological positions.

I was witness to an incident in which a young writer submitted to *Novy mir* his story about a priest. Everyone there warmly approved of it — in the distant 1960s this was an absolutely new theme. For understandable reasons, however, they could not publish it because the young author had painted a very sympathetic portrait of clergymen (perhaps he had some relative who was a priest). After agonizing a bit and losing hope that his story would ever be published, the young writer realized the problem and he submitted to *Novy mir* a different story about problems in the Church, this time from a critical perspective in which he unmasked greedy and sinful priests and cited some terrible facts. The prose section of the journal disapproved of the novice writer's verve and indignantly returned his manuscript, practically rebuking him for hypocrisy and dishonesty.

Publishing a story in those days about the life of the Church was in fact impossible and even inconceivable. The young writer had a poor grasp of the situation and wrote about what he knew best. He would have had equal success if he had written a novel about the life of prostitutes. The editors would have read it, but no one would have published it — neither the variant in which he pitied his heroines nor the opposite variant in which he condemned them for debauchery. Such themes as the Church, the sexual life of the Soviet people, to say nothing of repressions, the camps, the destroyed ecology, undermined health of the people, the problems of orphans, the elderly, single mothers, abandoned wives and children, the general lack and shortage of essential goods such as shoes or clothing (not to mention sausage or cheese, for which you stood in line for hours), and the horrible details of life of the ethnic minorities were all forbidden. Truth was in general forbidden.

Socialist Realism, the principal method in Soviet literature, presumed a certain romanticism manifested in an almost ideal portrayal of Soviet people and life. The most basic demand on the writer was to show a reverential attitude toward the Party and its leaders. The witty literary scholar Zinovy Paperny defined the method of Socialist Realism as "praise of the bosses in a form intelligible to them."

Our young hero, the novice prose writer, however, very much wanted to become a member of the Writers' Union. He had asked around and soon figured out the situation. He made the following move: he wrote a novel about progressive factory workers, and he very cleverly arranged for his manuscript to cross the desk of Georgy Markov, then First Secretary of the Writers' Union. That did the trick! Markov, a ludicrous figure who had long since forgotten how to write and fabricated novels about the lives of our "wingless angels" (i.e. Party leaders), read this fresh work, was delighted by this influx of new forces into literature and immediately sent the novel to the publishers. Then he admitted our hero into the Writers' Union, sent him on a junket to Siberia and then abroad, to Afghanistan, to begin with, where with the assistance of airplanes, tanks, infantry, and the lives of Russian boys we were helping the Afghan people advance toward their happy future, the rule of the Taliban. Our hero sat right down and wrote a novel about Afghanistan. To encourage him further they sent him to some embattled pro-Communist African country, and on instructions from the Party and the KGB he wrote a novel about this as well. He proved to be a very capable writer, and his literary career became radiant and clear: he became editor of an anti-Semitic periodical.

I mention this story to show that in Soviet times anyone with a strong desire and at least two years of elementary school could become a writer.

As a child I very much liked Soviet literature, since the libraries didn't have anything else. I read these enormous novels with pleasure (I did not know at the time that the authors were padding the page count to boost their fees). I literally devoured books on agriculture, metallurgical factories, and the peoples of the North, historical novels about Georgian princes, multi-volume works on the Russo-Japanese war and — especially — epics about the struggle of foreign Communists for their people's right to build socialism in Paris or Berlin. Getting hold of a spy novel was an unbelievable stroke of good luck! Believing that children need sleep my mother sometimes became angry and tried to take away these big heavy bricks of books that I would hide under my pillow to read at night. She didn't realize that she was interrupting the self-education of a writer, which was impossible without first reading pulp. I knew all about steel-making, including terms such as "cupola oven" and "silica clay"; I was well versed in agriculture and knew the times for sowing and harvesting grain and that milkmaids wore white smocks. I also understood the details of inner Party life and could distinguish the first secretary of a regional committee from the first secretary of a district committee.

As a child I was a well-educated Young Pioneer.

My attitude toward books was that I had to read whatever I happened to get hold of. Nothing put me off — not sluggish plots, or idiotic language, or cardboard characters. After school I did not go home for lunch or to play in the courtyard, but to the children's library. When it closed I dragged myself to the local "Party room" at the district Party headquarters on Chekhov Street; it was a dusty room with a carafe of water on the table, it was open to everyone (no one ever went there except me and a few guys who would play chess there when it was unusually cold outside), and in this building there was a cabinet with books and journals. I had read them all long ago, but I would sigh and pick out some enormous tome and dive into it again. I didn't care what it was as long as I could be reading. I knew *Krokodil* and *Ogonyok* practically by heart, unaware that many years later I would be publishing in them.

When I finished school I continued to visit my children's library all summer as I prepared to enter the university. And although the hardened lady librarians were strict with me (they refused to give me spy novels, demanding that I read books in the school curriculum), one of them was moved when I came to say goodbye after enrolling in Moscow University. She got out my completed library card, crossed out the first page with my name on it, turned it over in her hands without looking at me and suddenly said: "You know, you've read more books than anyone in the entire history of this library. We keep track. Drop by and see us occasionally."

I read the whole of Soviet literature — all the classics: Gorky's monstrous work *Mother* (*Mat'*) about raising the consciousness of a woman proletarian, and Pavlenko's no less awful novel *Happiness* (*Schastie*) in the final paragraph of which the hero and the heroine lie down in a rowboat and SHE says: "We'll name our son Iosif" (I always felt like adding "Vissarionovich"). I read the enormous novel *The Zhurbins*

(*Zhurbiny*) by I don't remember whom, *Alitet Goes to the Mountains* (*Alitet ukhodit v gory*) by another writer whose name I've forgotten, Galina Nikolaeva's *The Harvest* (*Zhatva*) about collective farms, and her book about steel workers, and I sincerely disliked Fadeev because both of his novels had unhappy endings. I only acknowledged happy endings, so I liked Fedin's two-volume work whose title I can't recall, and somewhere in Leonid Leonov I read and remembered the phrase: "He licked the spoon, and had five-fold more lips." That struck me as a clever turn of speech. I mused on it, and right then and there I suddenly understood what linguistic artifice was all about, realizing that there before me, perhaps, was a verbal masterpiece. I had never encountered anything like it before. Then I decided that Mayakovsky was a genius. I was fourteen at the time, the age at which young people usually begin to be interested in poetry. It suddenly struck me that you couldn't just knock together such rhymes! And that even with great effort, I was not going to achieve anything of the sort. So he was not like me and the rest of us: he was a genius!

Thus I grew up among terrible literature that I understood thoroughly and that did not demand the least intellectual effort. I swallowed those books the way a fish swallows water, or the way today's television viewer swallows the daily battery of soap operas. For neither Platonov, nor Babel, nor Bulgakov were permitted. The peaks of literature were hidden in the thick Party fog or buried beneath the murky waves of a Communist tsunami, as were buried the souls of millions of people who were bearers of a different culture and morality.

By the time I was an adolescent only the great foreigners were permitted. Not all of them. Not Kafka or Proust. But

Thomas Mann, Hemingway, Fitzgerald. It was as though a dam had burst deep within me. I realized that Thomas Mann would be my guide. And when I began to write myself I already knew that my sentences would be endless like his, they would meander and flow, steal up to the main point from the side, not head-on and not immediately.

Then suddenly something struck right at my heart — I became acquainted with Olesha, Shklovsky, and Tynyanov. Their theory of estrangement conquered my heart. Yes! From the very first sentence you have to amaze your readers and sweep them off their feet. You have to work on metaphors, on similes! I wrote my first story so ingenuously, stuffing several images into every sentence. Made-up eyelashes were like cockroach feet, a commuter train lowered its helmet and rushed on, an ice-cream wrapper puckered out like a ballet tutu, and so on.

All of this, however, was a preparatory stage. I was apparently searching for my own path, my own style. That's where it was heading. For years and years I worked in vain on my texts, writing and writing on the typewriter in the evening instead of going home. At the time I was working at a little magazine. In the humorous New Year's wall newspaper there were notes on who had accomplished what, and they wrote about me that I'd broken the letter "P" on the office typewriter!

But then our sound technician Zina told me a story about a neighbor of hers, a former prostitute who had been raped as a child by her father, she had left home and fallen into bad company. This story shook me.

I wrote "This Little Girl" (Takaya devochka). I wrote it very simply, without any special verbiage or images. It was not exactly the story of a former victim of a pedophile but a monologue of a woman whose husband was unfaithful to her. For some reason that is how it turned out. It was as though the short story wrote itself. And it didn't need any special style or editing. It determined how I would work from then on. Ever since then I have been writing as simply as possible, not specially trying to create something interesting, vivid, different. The stories followed effortlessly one after the other without questions, problems or pauses. It was as though someone were dictating them to me.

So to return to my reading as a child: understandably, over time my tastes had changed greatly, and I had begun to be interested in what my childhood reading had lacked, namely colloquial language, street talk.

Perhaps the difference between what I read in my childhood and real life was too great.

In the final analysis this cultivation of the ideal human being through textbooks of the ideal life yielded strikingly powerful results. The librarians had wanted to teach me to live according to the example of literary heroes who preached that you must never lie or dissemble but must stand up for your views no matter what. And that if you are a spy in the enemy camp, hold out to the very end.

And they made me into a fiery, honest, principled and implacable enemy of this literature and this order.

Like a veteran spy, however, I hid my real self for many years; I didn't make speeches, I didn't call press conferences when they wanted to arrest me, I wasn't a dissident, and I refused to emigrate.

And up until now I have not revealed this secret of mine.

So the above may be considered my first confession.

Nina SADUR

"I haven't yet fulfilled myself. I haven't realized all the talent God has granted me. And I must do so, otherwise I'll simply explode."

Nina Nikolaevna Sadur was born on 15 October 1950 in Novosibirsk. She has been writing short stories and plays since the late 1970s, publishing her first work in the journal *Sibirskie ogni* in 1977. In 1983 she graduated from the Moscow Literary Institute, where she attended the seminar of Victor Rozov and Inna Vishnevskaya.

Her first collection of plays, *The Odd Broad*, appeared in 1989 with an afterword by Rozov and gained her a certain recognition in literary and theater circles. Many of her popular plays, such as *The Odd Broad* (*Chudnaya baba*, 1981), *Group of Comrades* (*Gruppa tovarishchey*; 1982), *Drive On!* (*Yekhay!* 1984), and *Pannochka* based on Gogol (1985) date from the first half of the 1980s. She is also the author of several novels: *The Diamond Valley (Almaznaya Dolina), Miraculous Signs of Salvation* (*Chudesnye znaki spaseniya*), *The Garden* (*Sad*), and *The German* (*Nemets*), which are included in her collection *The Garden* (1997).

Of special interest are Sadur's experiments in the genre of erotic fiction published in the journal *Cats-show* (2001), some of which are collected in the book *Permafrost* (*Vechnaya merzlota*; 2002).

She is the 1997 winner of the *Znamya's* literary prize, and has written scripts for the television films *His Woman's Men* (*Muzhchiny ego zhenshchiny*) and *Me – That's You* (*Ya – eto ty*).

I'll never forget my first meeting with you as a writer and playwright. It was in 1987 when your play The Odd Broad was staged at the Yermolov Theater. *There were all sorts of reactions in the audience — enthusiasm, puzzlement, aggressiveness. How do you remember those days and that production?*

I remember — not everything, but I remember. I think that society wasn't ready for these plays. Plays that today appear traditional — such as *The Odd Broad* or *Drive On!* — seemed innovative then; and people don't know how to take innovation, anything out of the ordinary, it arouses fear and consequently aggression. The public then was generally sophisticated literarily and culturally. We were raised on our traditional Russian literature and on Soviet literature, in which, as is becoming clear to me now, there were a lot of good things. I ignored it the whole time, but now I am discovering some names for myself. And then this was an atheistic society that did not acknowledge any manifestations of the mystical world. I think that is why there was such aggressiveness.

Did you feel it?

I did. At Moscow University Theater Yevgeny Slavutin did a fine production of *The Odd Broad*. Afterwards he sat me on a chair on stage and the audience literally pounced on me. Some were shouting "How dare you?! That's no way to write!" I remember in my student days, when I'd written this play and someone — can't even remember his name, some instructor — shouted that I should be sent to an insane asylum. An instructor about a student, can you imagine? "You can't write like that! That's not the way to write! There are no plays like that!"

You said that there were many good things in Soviet culture. Are there any works of Soviet literature that still mean something to you?

Yes indeed, many of them. For example, I discovered Victor Astafiev. A few years ago the Krasnoyarsk Drama Theater commissioned me to write a play for his anniversary celebration. I chose his greatest, most frightening and powerful novel *The Damned and the Dead* (*Proklyatie i ubitye*), which presents his view of the Great Patriotic War (WWII) in which he served as a private in the signal corps. At the time he published this novel he ran into a lot of nastiness. The novel simply killed him. Everyone hated him for it; they took reprisals and persecuted him. But I was fascinated by this reality of a common soldier in that monstrous war of ours, where behind the frontlines almost twice as many people died as in the war itself. He is in a deep sense a profound, purely Russian writer who describes the world straightforwardly, movingly, and wisely. I simply fell in love with him, and now he'll always be my favorite. He hated the Communists and often said so. He was really sharp, a true Siberian.

Nina, you yourself were born in Siberia. Was it there you began writing?

I was destined to begin writing. I've talked about this

many times, but I think I was saying all sorts of silly things —
about childhood, this, that, and the other. It's my disposition, my
inner disposition. A confluence of circumstances, upbringing,
the awareness since I was a child that I must discover the
world, evaluate it, and tell about it. If they paid more attention
to my education, if someone had taken me in hand, perhaps I
could've become an artist. I don't know. It's just that my
father was a writer, a professional poet, and my mother was
a teacher of Russian literature. And there were a lot of books
in my life, in my childhood, at a time when there was a terrible
shortage of books in the Soviet Union. I had a wild imagination
and an individual way of seeing things. All of this makes a
writer.

*And yet all this was there in Siberia. Why did you
have to move to Moscow?*

You know, the time came. In fact, Victor Rozov, my future
teacher, urged me to come. We met at the Dubulti writers'
resort, he read my works and liked them very much. He kept
urging me to come to Moscow, but for several years I really
didn't want to go. Then I suddenly saw these faces around
me, and the rather closed world of writers there, and something
somehow clicked in my head. I realized that with my vision
of the world and the way I write I simply would never make
it as a writer in that conservative, narrow world.

*How do you imagine your artistic life had you
remained in Siberia?*

I don't know. I'd probably remain unknown, but I probably
wouldn't have stopped writing. I visited Siberia recently. My
goodness! A desert showered by the rain. That was me.

The rain — you mean here in Moscow?

The rain was Siberia. And I was the desert that began

flowering. It was on Lake Baikal, where I'd never been before. I simply fell in love. There I was cured of some sort of spiritual infirmities. It's a blessed land; Siberia is rich in talents.

And almost all of them come here.

But we don't know the ones who stay. I think that's how it happens — terribly, tragically, and uglily: mighty talents are born, but they don't find opportunities for growth, or support and willpower, perhaps. Most importantly, the growth they need. And since gifted people are radically different and deviate from the norm, they simply destroy themselves in their life situations. What is genius? Self-fulfillment? It is powerful, powerful talent plus willpower and circumstances. You have to have an irresistible attraction to your calling. Siberia is unbelievably talented genetically, because for three hundred years all the best, everything offbeat, everything that didn't conform to generally accepted norms was sent into exile there. Siberia, after all, is called Russia's America.

What kind of a reception did you get in Moscow?

I think I was received well. The Literary Institute was simply a marvelous place for people like me. The whole time I was there I felt love and tolerance of me and my pranks. Overall I think they even spoiled me there. They allowed me things that simply horrify me today. The Institute, of course, was unique. But today, under Yesin... Yesin turned it into a vocational school. If people are themselves untalented and envious, everything around them becomes dead and gray.

Let's talk about Gogol's influence. I know that you don't like labels, but still, you have been living for some time next to the building in which Gogol spent his last years. Does that mean anything to you?

The first years here I lived on that alone. Especially a mystical coincidence just after I arrived when the Lenkom director Mark Zakharov called me and asked me to write a play based on *Dead Souls*. It's a few minutes walk from my previous home to my present one. There I wrote *Pannochka* under the strangest circumstances, and here I did *Dead Souls*. I experienced serious emotional shocks in connection with Gogol, in connection with the play, in connection with the fact that I was living near his home. But now I've calmed down.

You've been living here for some time, after all.

I've been living here a long time, and I've gone through many different inner states because of it. And what shocks me is that people around me, who live near him as I do, don't know what he wrote. They live close by just like me, but that's it.

You've already mentioned plays on Gogolian motifs. How many have you done?

Two based on Gogol. I also have plays based on other writers. People say that I've discovered an entire genre — motif plays. "Dramatizations" are a different genre, and I've been asked to do some, but I can't. I have my own thoughts and vision, so I started writing plays about how I imagine the story of another writer, and I called them "motif plays." And now there are so many of them that they are a genre of their own. After *Pannochka* came a whole stream of "motif" plays.

Gogol, of course, is more congenial to you than the Latin American magic realists.

Much more congenial. Gogol is closer than the magic realists of Latin America to all Russian writers if only because they share the Russian language and — to use a fashionable word — the mentality. Gogol saw right through the Russian essence. By some animal instinct he sensed the slightest movements in this nature of ours, that boundlessness that sometimes makes you want to blow this country up. I sometimes hate my people for being like that.

I remember how, at the time your novel **The Garden** *appeared, you suffered for the poor of Russia.*

I've calmed down already. I have a lot of reasons to suffer. They've died, quite simply, they are no more. Now we have classic bums, the kind that exist all over the world. They are very clearly delineated socially. They don't want to work, or circumstances are such that they can't, but mostly they don't want to. And so they sink lower, and lower, and lower. The bums and beggers that were here before have simply died out. Those little children who swarmed all over before are no more.

When we first met you firmly denied any influence from the European absurdists.

I've just now finally read Ionesco. It's the first time I've read his play *Rhinoceros*. Do you really think that I have something in common with him? In that case I don't understand the meaning of the word "absurdism." His play has a thoroughly logical structure. It's a parable play — logically designed, traditional in form, well written. It's nicely done, polyphonic, with a very interesting structure, but this is quite traditional drama. So we have to agree on the terminology. The absurd is alogical whereas the parable is structured on iron logic. That's the story — draw your own conclusions.

You, of course, work with alogism.

Exactly. Now this play *Rhinoceros*, — seeing as how

I've been commissioned to write *Rhinoceros-2* for the Bolshoi Drama Theater in St Petersburg — is a parable. Whereas Beckett — yes. It's subtle. A subtle game. *Waiting for Godot* — I adore this play. But it too is just a mind game. One thought battles another.

You also play such games.

Yes, I do. I suppose even Beckett is closer to me. But Ionesco — sorry. That said, I like Ionesco very much. Just now I'm writing a play based on him — his structure, his idea, but set in contemporary Russian reality.

It's been said that your prose must be read like poetry. What is the secret of your style? How do you work? I see a sheet of paper over there, so you write longhand.

My typewriter — my little friend — is broken. I've written all my life on that typewriter, but I like writing longhand. How do I work? Now I work differently somehow. I went through a major creative crisis, or rather a personal crisis. Well, both. When I saw how unruly life in our culture was becoming I fell into despair and a very deep depression. Society is going wild. And then I suddenly realized: why shouldn't it run wild? For seventy years we lived with Communism's satanic ideas. Then all of that collapsed and we lapsed into utter savagery. This wildness is the result of the fateful crimes of our society. I think I'm entering a new phase of my artistic development, and therefore I've begun writing differently somehow and seeing differently, but I still haven't put it into words.

You mentioned depression and that sometimes you hate the Russian people?

Of course. And why do I hate them? They are the only people I have.

The Garden *is a genuinely polyphonic novel. It has many themes, but the most important thing, I think, is your mythological interpretation of the collapse of the Soviet Union.*

Yes, that's there. So you noticed it? I'm so intimidated by our critics that when anyone notices anything, I'm so grateful to them. Although these are utterly obvious things, aren't they? You know, it was very beautiful. It was like a garden. Like a garden shedding its greenery — an image of our totalitarian state and empire. Do you know how people lived? Here's how they lived. The cage opened, the birds all jumped out, but they still don't know that they can't fly.

Is there a tragedy there?

Don't think that the tragedy is only in my works. Our whole country has been sick. It's just that I know how to express it and put it into words. The man on the street doesn't express anything. He formulates his everyday needs, but hardly any greater ones.

In **The Garden** *there are genuine tragedies, but also sorrow. And it seems to me that the comfort is snow — snow from Siberia.*

I love snow. I've missed it so much in Moscow. I'm a Siberian, after all. And in Siberia snow is something special, like a kind of holiday. It's a philosophy, God, happiness, joy. And its also danger and death. Everything together. Snow is why people in Siberia are so tall, strong, and handsome. In Siberia there are very handsome people; the whole Siberian people is beautiful. I'm probably nostalgic for my birthplace.

In this same novel you describe marginal people. Is there a place for them today in Moscow and in your writing?

Oh yes. Beginning with the fact that not only in Russia, in any society, artists are the number one marginals. Kings of the marginals, otherwise they aren't artists. The others are their subjects who merely exist, but they as kings have to watch over hostile territories. And that is essentially what I do.

But Nina, what about the PEN Club, and the writers' organizations?

I have a very lively relationship with the PEN Club, but as for writers' organizations such as Litfond... I waited in line for around fifteen years for a stupid dacha in Peredelkino. I had nowhere at all to work and wanted to write there, because there are two writers in the family — me and my daughter Katya[9]. Then someone by the name of Ognev threw out my application and they said that they didn't have it. And they give these dachas to who knows whom — widows, officials.

Germany is often mentioned in contemporary Russian literature. What does the German theme mean for you? I'm thinking of your novel **The German.**

That novel is based on my impressions of Berlin. It was a mystical trip. Very. A strange trip, and I met some strange people. A very difficult trip. I think that I sensed what I later began to learn about Berlin. I don't know whether it's a superstition or a legend, but when the Nazis abandoned Berlin — and they practiced black magic, just like our Communists...

Black magic... You're speaking metaphorically?

Not at all. When the Nazis abandoned Berlin, they put a

---

[9] Yekaterina Sadur, Nina Sadur's daughter, a young prose writer and playwright, winner of the journal *Znamya*'s literary prize.

satanic curse on it. This is a legend, but it has been documented that Hitler and the SS were interested in the Cabala and black magic. Exactly like our Communists. They studied these things and practiced rituals. When I was there I seemed to sense some kind of powerful, very dark mystical currents. I wasn't able to figure it out, but I simply found myself in that element. And once I ran into a very strange person, a very strange young man.

A meeting between Russia and Germany, if you will.

Not a simple meeting... My generation was born of parents who were half-killed by Germany. I still remember this in my genes. And at the same time everything is already over. There is some kind of link, a bloody, blood link on that level, and on that level something is still emerging.

Quite apart from society, your heroes often find themselves in crisis in a sick world. Are you particularly interested in liminal states?

Yes. I'm not interested in reading matter for the average reader — stories with measured doses of emotions. I'm interested in taking a soul at a moment of crisis, when all of its properties, its personality, are laid bare. You know, like solar eruptions on the sun. This is the state of the hero. In each individual there slumbers a hero, and the state of the hero in a person is also my state "after the hero." The hero always dies, of course. In folk tales and myths the hero always perishes, and I understand why. Because he also perishes in real life. A person performs a heroic act but he can't hold on to it his whole life. And all that remains after him is a burnt-out shell sinking, always sinking. All his subsequent life he pays for his heroism, for sticking out of the crowd. That's what I find interesting in people.

In **The Garden** *you are one of the first Russian women writers to take up the profoundly Russian theme of hard drinking.*

It's simply that I know the subject and had a warm spot in my heart for this problem. But you'll agree that the state my characters are in is pleasant — it's so carnivalesque, so comfy. When ordinary people go on a binge it's one thing, but when gifted, colorful people in love with each other do it, it's a celebration.

At some point you said that there are only two themes in literature: the relationship between man and woman and the relationship between man and God. Everything else is just plots.

The relationship between God and man is the main theme. There is no other theme. We are all moving toward God, after all. People travel different roads and can refuse to go there, but a meeting is inevitable.

Yet we encounter sorcerers in your works more often than we do God.

Do you know what sorcerers are? They are little ruffians who don't want to study but want to know everything all at once.

I see. And that is why things don't turn out so well for them.

Yes, and God is looking at them while they think they are so clever.

But there is no open religiosity in your works.

No. I'm not a churchgoer. I don't even know much about religion. I was born in Soviet times, after all. I was baptized in Orthodoxy and I believe that we are moving toward God. As for my daughter Katya and granddaughter Aglaya, they belong to the church. Aglaya goes to Sunday school. We have a very good congregation, with decent, wonderful priests, wonderful children and teachers. We're lucky that such things are happening here.

Quite a few of your stories are dedicated to relationships among women. Those young girls, for example, who come to work in Moscow. They associate mostly with their girlfriends and old women in the communal apartment, where there is a real drama, right?

People do not exist in a vacuum. They are not hermits. The chosen are granted direct communication with God, but I'm not among them. I have a different role. I live in the world among people; I influence them, they influence me. My heroes wander through life communicating with whomever fate brings them. As for the relationship between man and woman, I meant love. The strongest human emotional experience on this earth is being in love.

Yet you have a special women's world: young girls, malicious old women, and then there are the sorcerers and magic. Where does this magic come from?

The magic is from the communal apartment, where my "Motherland" settled me to sing her praises forever. I lived in a communal apartment that cannot be compared with anything else the world has produced. I observed corrupted personalities that I cannot imagine even in Dante's *Inferno*. The communal apartment is Stalin's invention. Lives intertwine.

So this is the structure of the communal apartment.

You should have seen the people who live there. The one where I lived had one woman who was a jailbird thief, an old Jewish grandmother, a hunchback spinster, a rather decent and healthy couple on temporary work permits and their daughter, married to an Armenian who worked for the KGB. And me, absolutely incomprehensible to them all.

In Russia today there is enormous interest in all sorts of metaphysical things: extrasensory perception, black magic, etc. What's your opinion of all this?

Extremely negative. I detest it. That goes for sectarianism also. I think that sectarianism is a crime that the state disregards. Or else they don't understand that it's irreversible. Teenagers get into it and in ten years or so they will have to atone for all the rest of their lives. This is a symptom of the decay and rot in our society, which is in a terrible state of degradation spiritually and culturally, and it gets worse day by day. It's simply horrible the things that are proclaimed to be our cultural heritage.

Nina, do you think that there is such a thing as women's prose?

This is something the critics have invented and made a fashion of sorts. I think that it's a silly fabrication, however, because it's simply shameful the features they use to define women's prose. It is literature of very poor quality entirely focused on the sexual relations between men and women. Women, at any rate, deserve more.

What problems or themes are you concerned about today?

I'm awake now and I've become strong and mature enough to tackle social problems. Not only that, but I've realized that this is a highly interesting area, and I've even discovered that I'm something of a political pamphleteer. If not pamphlets, then at least something on critical social issues. And soon I'll be regaling you with it. Our bigwigs are doing such terrible things to our people, to Moscow — they've stripped it bare.

Will you be able to write about this? Stories? Plays?

I'm trying to. It's my first attempt. If it doesn't go through, I'll send it to you. It's all based on Ionesco's *Rhinoceros*.

Yes, you said that it is set in Russia.

It's set in a fictitious provincial city that is a replica of Russia. What is going on in Russia today will also happen in the play. All of the social ills we see today — everything will be in it.

I believe you're also working for television?

I'm writing screenplays — for money. But I've really come to like it. We have a good group there. Well, the cultural level is quite low, of course, as everywhere, in all spheres of cultural activity. We've written a series that hasn't been produced yet consisting of scenes from provincial life centering on a humble district doctor, a therapist who goes from house to house, and through him we show the life of the town. It's a good series.

I read that in your series **The Woman Taxi Driver (Taksistka)** *you mainly "put various stories from the life of a woman behind the wheel into a literary form."*

I was in charge of the script of this series, meaning that it was my job to keep track of everything, and then I wrote a few episodes. I really like this series. I only worked on the first block. There was a second and a third, but by then I was no longer working there.

And then you also published in the pornographic magazine **Cats-show.** *What were those stories like?*

Let's not talk about them. It's a terrible magazine. I don't even remember what they were.

For money?

Of course. Then I published my book *Permafrost* (*Vechnaia merzlota*).

In the West you are known as a playwright and prosaist, and you've been translated into many languages. Here in Russia your plays are produced by the Bolshoi Theater in Petersburg and published. But it's a complete mystery to me why the Russian critics of postmodernism write so little about you, and that you haven't been given any prizes or even a dacha in Peredelkino. What is your own view of this?

My friends and colleagues have tried to explain the problem to me. It has to do with personalities. You have to be in the right place at the right time. You have to get to know the right people. I don't. And I don't resemble them in my writing either. They simply don't know what to do with it. Critics, after all, are self-serving. They take a writer on their own level of development and promote him/her. Critics go for writers of the same level of education, culture, and talent as themselves. And evidently I just don't lend myself to their analysis. They simply don't understand what I am.

And the last question, Nina. After you've worked on television and popular magazines how do you view the role of genuine literature today in competition with the other mass media?

In competition with the other mass media it loses. Serious literature loses completely. The Russian they teach at schools! Some sort of enemy saboteurs wrote those textbooks! In our Russian literature textbooks Pushkin isn't even mentioned. If it weren't for the family, the children would run wild. They are studying our second and third-rate contemporary poets.

Or they just up and take Kharms entirely out of the context of OBERIU.[10] Kharms is an innovator of the Russian language. In the beginning children should learn classical Russian, shouldn't they? All right — Kharms is a genius, so he can be explained to children at home. But when they parrot Chukovsky's *Doctor Ouch*! (*Doktor Ay-bolit*). When they study Astrid Lindgren as Russian literature, what they're studying is not Astrid Lindgren, but the translator.

---

[10]OBIERU (The Association of Real Art) – a short-lived avant-garde group founded in 1928 by Kharms and others that is considered to have foreshadowed the European Theater of the Absurd.

Mikhail SHISHKIN

Ivonne Boeler

"I try to make each work a total text that absorbs all previous culture and literature".

Mikhail Pavlovich Shishkin was born in Moscow on 18 January 1961. He has at various times worked as a school teacher, a journalist, and a translator.

His first novel *The Same Night Awaits Us All* (*Vsekh ozhidaet odna noch*), (*Znamya*: 1993) was awarded the journal's prize for best debut work of the year, and it is in *Znamya* that Shishkin's subsequent novels — *The Taking of Izmail* (*Vzyatie Izmaila*; 1999) and *Hair of Venus* (*Venerin volos*, 2005) — first appeared.

For family reasons he has been living in Switzerland since 1995, where he has worked as an interpreter in the immigration service.

For *The Taking of Izmail* he received the 2000 Russian Booker Prize. In France, the French translation of *Montreux-Missolunghi-Astapovo: In the Footsteps of Byron and Tolstoy* (originally published in German) was awarded the prize for the best foreign book of 2005, and in the same year he received the

Booker Prize in the essay category and the National Bestseller Prize for *Hair of Venus*. In 2006 he won the Big Book Award, and a play based on *Hair of Venus* was staged in Moscow under the direction of Pyotr Fomenko.

Where does your interest in literature come from? What part did school and your family play? Your mother taught Russian literature, did she?

I think then literature played a much different role than it does now. My ten-year-old son is Swiss and he basically doesn't read either in German or in Russian, although he can read in both languages. But he doesn't feel the same need as my older son, who is now eighteen. When I was ten and eighteen, we lived at the bottom of a thick leather sack, so to speak, and had no possibility whatever of getting cultural information; we were cut off from the rest of the world and had only stale "Soviet air" to breathe. The only books were those that were officially permitted, and except for books there was practically nothing -- no television, no radio, no music. Cultural information was accessible only in the form of the printed word. Although my mother was a literature teacher, I don't think she influenced me. Instead it was probably my older brother, who was bringing me forbidden books, and that strong wave of cultural influence had some effect. Right away, of course, there was fighting on the "barricades," because Mama was a Party member and a school principal. So there was a "rebellion" in the family — the son against his parents. My father and mother had separated, so he was not a problem. Eighteen is an age when you want to show your independence. It's when you first have to vote — the first time you're tested to see whether you'll sell your soul to the devil. My brother, of course, raised a ruckus. It was a terrible thing for my mother to have her son throwing a political scene. You can just imagine — this was in the seventies! And I was alongside him there on the "barricades" because my childish heart sided with him rather than her. As things turned out, I began to associate with his friends, who were like gods to me. I would sit silently in a corner and listen to their intelligent, freedom-loving conversations, where I heard names I otherwise never would have heard.

For example?

Brodsky, Nabokov, Mandelstam — I got to know all of them through my brother. I think that this truly was the beginning. I started off by saying that literature played an entirely different role back then. If there hadn't been this "vent," without this possibility to breathe different air through books, life would have been humiliating. Living in the Soviet Union was generally humiliating. Reading forbidden books was the only way to find a niche where you were not being constantly put down but on the contrary were raised up. This was how you preserved your human dignity. I began writing much earlier, of course. Here you probably have to distinguish between consciously or unconsciously becoming a writer. You have to be crazy to become a writer as an adult, but as a child you don't ask yourself such questions. You take a sheet of paper and write on it: "A Novel." I, for example, wrote my first novel when I was nine, I remember it very well, and I describe it in *The Taking of Izmail.* You should be able to find the episode, it's literally copied from reality: at our summerhouse one day I pick up a notebook and write a novel.

Further on, however, once you've written your novel, you expect to have readers. It goes without saying that my grandmother with her three years of parish school couldn't be considered a reader, so I waited for my mother to come home from work. She came, and I said: "Mama, look, I've written a novel!" I remember very well her exclaiming: "Oh, Misha wrote a novel!" She smiled cheerfully enough, but if she'd said: "Oh, Misha mopped the floor!" she would have been just as cheerful. I watched her as she began reading, and then she frowned and looked serious and dissatisfied. A single frowning glance from her could pacify a rowdy class at school — it immediately gave you goose bumps. And she said to me in a very serious, displeased tone of voice: "Misha, you should only write about things you understand." She expected a novel about Indians or some science fiction — about aliens and adventures, but it was about divorce, because my mother and father seemed to be eternally getting divorced before my very eyes, and what I saw before me is what I described. Ever since then I think that the family theme has run like a red thread through all my works, and I'm always writing about things that I don't know and don't understand.

In spite of your mother's negative criticism, however, your path to literature seems unusually straight. Your training is not as an engineer, but as a philologist, and you were immediately noticed and appreciated as a writer. Was it in fact like that?

I don't think that I came straight into literature. I was always writing, but I deliberately chose to write only things that could not be published in the Soviet world. In that sense my path to literature was straight, because it was easy for me to reject the conventionalities or rules of the game that I refused to accept. The literature that existed then did not satisfy me at all. Especially stylistically, and even those forbidden works I had the incentive to read. For instance, someone lends you Voinovich's *The Life and Extraordinary Adventures of Private Chonkin* (*Zhizn i neobychaynye priklyucheniya soldata Ivana Chonkina*) for one night and you read it because you have to, but you don't like it anyway, because it's written in the Soviet style — in the style of the new world that you reject. It is flesh of the flesh of the totalitarian Soviet consciousness turned inside out, and this comes through in the style. Working on style, searching for something new and important through language was for me from the outset simply a necessity of life. When I was sixteen I read Sasha Sokolov's *School for Fools* (*Skhola dlya durakov*), which had just come out in America and found its way to Russia, heaven knows how, and it made an overwhelming impression on me.

Just imagine a man living in a world where writers are like gods to him. All the gods lived back in the nineteenth century, however, and what he reads now, what is being published now, has nothing godlike or sacred about it. Suddenly along comes a book that shows him the way: yes, there is something sacred; in spite of everything you can find something godlike through the word. I wrote the whole time with no hope of ever being published in the Soviet Union. Perhaps sometime, somewhere, if I wrote something worthwhile, it might be published in the West. I always had this idea somewhere deep in my mind, but it wasn't important; what I needed to begin with was just to write something — something that I myself could be satisfied with; something in which I myself felt I'd said something new. As it seemed to me, of course, everything I wrote wasn't quite right. My first novel wasn't quite it, either, so I abandoned it. The first time I thought I'd accomplished something was my story *The Calligraphy Lesson (Urok kaligrafii)*, which I wrote some time back around 1989 or 1990. Before that I hadn't thought of publishing anything, especially because when perestroika began, there was a huge backlog of everything that could not be published during the seventy years of the Soviet regime. It would have been ridiculous and naïve to try to compete against them with my little story, so I didn't try. I patiently kept on waiting for something to be published sometime. That it happened in 1993 is probably logical, since by then the bulk of unpublished works had already appeared, and the journals — at that time most publishing was in journals — had again started searching for new names in contemporary literature.

And then right away **Znamya** *awarded your first novel its prize for the best literary debut.*

Yes, *Znamia* gave me the prize for the best debut of the year for my story *The Calligraphy Lesson* and my first novel.

Then you won two prestigious literary prizes: for your second novel **The Taking of Izmail** *you got the Russian Booker, and for the third,* **Hair of Venus,** *the National Bestseller award. Did this equal recognition help you to develop your own, individual writing manner?*

Recognition and whether it helped me is a very complex question. Quite frankly, I didn't give it any thought. I think I would have written the same whether I'd gotten a prize or not. As it turned out, all my works were published. I don't write much, however — one work every five years. Every time I finish a novel and send it to *Znamya*, I'm not sure they will accept it, because the basic trend today is toward easy reading — "Akuninism." Readable and accessible Akunin is like the lodestar of Russian literature. I'm moving in a different direction. I consciously do not strive for recognition, let alone, prizes, and I deliberately avoid making my works easy, so that every time I publish something or on top of that win an award, it's a surprise to me — a pleasant one, of course. But, as you put it, has recognition helped me? Perhaps. When you don't win a prize you think getting it is important, because it could solve some problems, help you economically, help you get published, and so on. But when you do get it you are free from this idea, because you see that nothing changes.

Since all of your books have won prizes, you're completely free...

I suppose you could also put it that way. But generally speaking, I think that you really have to get a prize in order to realize that you don't have to have it.

You mentioned Akunin, while the opinion not only of the public at large but also of many critics, is that you are difficult to read. One critic wrote about **The Taking of Izmail** *that it took him nine whole days to get through the first fifty pages. Another calls it a "Mecca for Logophiles", and a third declares outright: "No one is going to read Shishkin." Does such criticism upset you?*

In was important in the beginning what they wrote about me. These intelligent people who understand something about literature seemed to be saying important, intelligent things, and something in literature seemed to depend on these important, intelligent things. With published books, and time, and experience, you eventually realize that the critics have nothing at all to do with literature. Everything they say describes not the text but themselves. My latest novels, especially *Hair of Venus*, were given a hostile reception. I try not to read any of it any more, because it doesn't interest me at all. When I do read something and try to understand the hostility, however, the arguments I find are simply amazing. The main thrust of Yeliseev's article in *Novy mir,* for example, was that the writer is a Russian living abroad and therefore has no moral right to write about Russia. Do you understand? Discussions on such a level have nothing to do with literature or the novel. When critics declare that no one is going to read the book, and then suddenly it's on the bestseller list of all the Moscow bookstores for weeks — in the top ten together with Dan Brown and Coelho — when it sells out and is followed immediately by three editions in a row, then I don't care what the critics think.

You yourself say "I think that the reason Russian readers are interested in my works is that I give them back their dignity." What do you mean by that?

Critics who consider readability a criterion don't even exist for me, because they don't understand anything about literature. There's an anecdote about James Joyce where one of his female readers says to him: "You know, your book was so hard to read!" To which Joyce replied: "But you know, my book was so hard to write!" An approach that judges difficulty or ease of reading is no approach at all. The point has to do with a certain level of literary development that demands a certain level of education both of the writer and of the reader. If you don't speak Swedish, you can't just sit down and read Strindberg. You have to learn Swedish first. The same goes for any literary text: if you don't know world literature and haven't read a certain number of books, you cannot get pleasure from a book written on a certain level.

Putting words together gives me a kind of joy. And I'm sure there are intelligent, educated, well-bred, deeply sensitive people who feel the joy that comes from literature and words, and that is what I want to share with them. How many of them are there? Editions — whether in the millions (which I seriously doubt), or, say, twenty thousand, are quite a different matter. Why talk about editions? In Russia literature has become a means of making money, and the criterion has changed: if you have big editions, it's good literature; if you don't sell well, it's bad literature. I'm not happy with such criteria.

I was trying to ask you about something else — about giving Russian readers back their dignity. What do you mean by that?

What I mean is that in Russia, as I mentioned in the beginning, where reading was a way of preserving human dignity, the faith has changed, and everyone has begun believing in the dollar. As we say in Russian: "Make a fool pray, and he'll break his head bowing down." The whole country is breaking its head bowing down to the dollar. All the writers have rushed to earn money — temptation by bestseller, as it were — and they have entered into a tacit conspiracy with each other against the reader to lower the bar, lower the overall level. Readers form a pyramid, you understand, and the lower you put the bar the more readers or viewers you're going to have.

Thus there is this conspiracy against readers — yes, against ordinary people, who haven't disappeared and who go to a bookstore to find a book on their level, meeting their expectations, a book in which the author suffers and searches for God just like they do. And instead of that sought-after book, what they are offered is something fit for an idiot. This is insulting to them, as it would be insulting to me in their place, because the books I expect are completely different; I expect a different *feeling* or attitude toward me. I don't want to be taken for an idiot, and I'm insulted when that kind of literature is foisted on me.

Epochs and peoples, milieus and social strata, characters and historical prototypes, well known events and individual lives, fragments from the lives of others and your own reminiscences are all mixed together in your novels. One could say that these are novels about everything — an attempt to create a complete reality. Why is this global approach so important to you?

It's all a question of format. Why do you write a very short story, why do you write a gigantic novel? Before sitting down at the computer or picking up a pen, anyone who writes should have an idea of the format. Generally speaking, the format used by so-called "normal" writers is determined by the publisher: if you're writing for a journal or newspaper, obviously the text will tend to be short; if you're writing for a publishing house you are going to produce a certain standard quantity of printer's sheets — no more, no less. As for me, I don't write for publishers. The reason I write is to set something in contrast to the world in which I find myself. If this world is gigantic, huge and disharmonious, then I have to contrast it with something that is no less huge and gigantic, but harmonious. If in this world there are different times, states, people — everything you just enumerated — then it's like a boat: you have to load each side equally, because otherwise it will capsize! It's important for me to create a world that will balance this so-called real world, so that if it contains death, then to keep the boat from capsizing, on the other side you have to put immortality. A genius could get all of this into a short story. I'm not a genius, so I produce big novels into which I try to stuff everything, including immortality.

Your narrative structure is distinctive. Your works read like a polyphonic confluence of many voices with different intonations and discourses. They tell their stories, but they constantly interrupt each other. Surely this fragmentariness is not only postmodernist play?

I think the point here is much deeper than just play or stylistic devices or fragmentariness. Creating human images is implicitly based on the illusion that we are all different. What differentiates us, to use a sea metaphor, is merely foam, slight ripples, waves on the surface of the ocean. What unites us in the most profound sense, however, are kilometers of human depth. I have to remove this surface layer and extract the depth. The only reason I create images of different people and different times is at some point to reveal the illusion that they are different. In *Hair of Venus*, at least, I tried to. All of these different human voices ultimately converge in two male and female images: Daphne and Chloe, Tristan and Isolde, he and she, man and woman. This is what is important to me — not fragmentariness, but on the contrary, the harmonious union of everything with everything.

Meaning through fragments that unite. And you spoke of the depth we all share. **The Taking of Izmail,** *at any rate, is a Russian version of this depth, and both on the surface and deep down this Russian life seems more than anything to consist of savage cruelty and human suffering. I remember particularly vividly pages describing the hopeless and humiliating life of a cultural worker in some*

Godforsaken backwater. The impression from reading these dark pages is that life in Russia after the Revolution, at any rate, is not life but metaphysical suffering.

I think that *Izmail* is not about suffering as such, but about overcoming suffering. In the figurative sense the taking of Izmail has to do with the "taking," or "conquering" of this life. The hero's father says to him: "Mishka, you have to take this life as you would take a fortress." You're born into this world, and for me the world at that time was Russia. If you're born in Russia and have come face to face with its reality and past, you realize that you love this monstrous fatherland and have to accept life as it is. How to accept it, how to take it — that is what the novel is about. There are two parallel paths along which life can be overcome: through the birth of a child — that's one way to conquer life — and by creating a collection. The hero creates a collection; that is, he tries to create art out of the horrors by transforming them into words.

I ask myself the same question in each work: "What am I doing? What is prose? What is art?" Art is what conquers horrible reality. When a man is nailed alive to a cross, there is blood and pain — it's horrible. A normal person cannot stand to watch it, but from it beautiful works of art have been born. That is, a terrible experience is transformed into a sublime experience, into union with God. In this sense what *The Taking of Izmail* is about is overcoming terrible reality through sublime union with beauty and art. Art, the sublime, and beauty are the forms in which the divine exists.

There is also the matter of different levels. After all, you describe Russia as a "country where people have made a hell for themselves, a country in which everything has always obeyed a single law: might is right." The critic

Andrey Nemzer quotes you as saying "It's impossible to live in this country," and he adds: "This is a passionate attempt to justify the emigration of the 1990s." What's your reaction?

What he is saying describes not my novel, but where Russia has gone in the nineties. When my first novel came out, Nemzer's review was the best. He wrote a big article in *Nezavisimaya gazeta* called "Not Yet Evening" (Esche ne vecher), by which he meant that Russian literature was not yet dead, that if promising young names were still appearing, then Russian literature had a great future. Among these names, he prophesized, is Shishkin, who has appeared like a new star in the firmament...

What has happened since is interesting. Instead of opening up to the world and uniting with the world, in recent years Russia has been moving in the completely opposite direction: resurgent chauvinism, new delusions of grandeur alongside an unbelievable inferiority complex. Everything that is not in Russia, everything in the West, is once again the enemy. Once again Russia is looking at the world from the ramparts. Anyone not with us is against us. And to leave Russia for the West and live in the West is unpardonable! This started after *Izmail*, in an article in *Novy mir* entitled "Down the Down Staircase" (Vniz po lestnitse vedushchey vniz) where already then I was called a champion of Western influence in Russian literature. That's a charge that won't wash off! Something strange happened to Nemzer. He was an extremely intelligent man who went crazy together with the country. Now he's a patriot, and anyone who takes the liberty of criticizing Russia, especially anyone who lives in the West, is his personal enemy. Thus he considers that I am not a patriot and he is the patriot. Do you understand? Such a primitive level of consciousness!

It pains me to see what is going on in Russia. All of my works are declarations of love for Russia, so that when someone waves their "literary patriot" pedigree in my face and tells me that I don't have the right to declare either love or hatred of Russia, it grieves and disappoints me that such things are going on there. This is unworthy of Russia.

Forgive me for getting a bit excited. These things irritate me terribly. It is such a primitive level of consciousness. In Russia there is of course no such thing as political correctness.

I know.

So that whereas in Switzerland or Germany when critics want to criticize a book, they speak to the point without insulting you personally, in Russia they just throw mud at you, calling you — as Nemzer did me — "the Swiss Sage." If someone were to write such an article in Switzerland, no one would want to have anything to do with him because of his shameless behavior. In Russia shamelessness is the norm, and it has nothing to do with the works themselves.

To continue this theme, in your latest novel **Hair of Venus** *various times — antiquity, the early twentieth century, the present — run together, but there is also all the savagery of life in Russia: the Revolution, the Civil War, the camps, the army, the orphanages, criminal shootouts, the so-called sweep operations in Chechnya, and of course, all the horror of everyday life.*

In *Izmail* I was inside the Russian world, although I was already writing in Switzerland. The Russian world, however, is only a *tiny* piece of God's world. People inside Russia don't understand this. They think that Russia is the whole of God's world, but when you leave you realize that Russia is only a *tiny* part of God's world, and that besides Russia there is a great deal more. This is what Nemzer and his ilk can't forgive me in *Hair of Venus* — the fact that I write not only about Russia. In *Izmail* I was accused of writing badly about Russia from Switzerland. But now it's as though what is important to me is no longer Russia but the entire world, and that makes me a kind of traitor in their eyes. In *Hair of Venus*, in fact, I'm not interested in Russia as such or in Switzerland. I'm interested in deeper things: the birth of a human being, human love, the birth of children, death, and resurrection. This is a novel on a different level and about something else. The King Herod who devours children is not geography and not Russia. In *Izmail* it was in Russia that the conquest of life and overcoming the fear of life took place, so that Russia and the world were like a single whole. *Hair of Venus,* however, presents the broader concept that life is not only Russia, life is not only fear and is not at all to be feared — life is to be enjoyed. The King Herod devouring children is, in fact, time. What has to be struggled against is not Russia, but time. You have to do something to fight death. And people die not only in Russia.

Like The Taking of Izmail, Hair of Venus *was written in Switzerland, and you say that the idea for these novels came to you by way of the Alps. Do you think that you can see Russia better that way?*

Absolutely. Of course it helped me. I think that it is useful for any writer to leave; that it's absolutely necessary to get away. Earlier in the nineteenth century the Academy of Art in St Petersburg sent artists abroad to Italy not only to learn art techniques by looking at excavated ancient Roman statues and the ruins of the Colosseum and the paintings of the great masters. They left Russia in order to look at a different sky and different colors and to understand what the sky was like in Russia. As long as you are living in Russia and haven't visited Italy, you can't understand the colors of the sky. The same goes for writers. If they live only in Russia and write only about that world, they think that they know everything. They have to leave to understand that they know nothing. Least of all about Russia.

Hair of Venus *begins quite simply: an interpreter working in Zurich listens for months to the most horrible stories from Russian refugees. How important is the documentary background in the novel?*

What does that mean — "important"?! It's the main thing. A text is a metaphor, but metaphors must be based on reality. There has to be a point of reference or a jumping-off point. Reality is the lever with which Archimedes wanted to lift the world. By pushing off from this reality and transforming and metaphorizing it, I begin to construct my own world, my own reality. If the other reality does not exist, then it is impossible to construct an alternative one.

The development of the question-answer format is interesting and original. The reader can't be sure who is right, who is asking the questions, who has the real power.

Well, this is my reality, the material out of which I begin to build. Moreover, this reality asks what art is: you sit and listen to stories, and you never know whether they are invented or true. And this is what *Hair of Venus* is about — those horrible stories told by the two young men that begin the novel. Then it suddenly turns out that these stories are not theirs — they have made them up or heard them somewhere. So you come to the question "What is art?" If you are telling a terrible story that didn't actually happen or happened to someone else, is it real or not? This is where it begins to be interesting, and this is where the novel begins as well.

You say that your novels demand considerable effort to write. What about your books of essays? You were writing **The Taking of Izmail** *and* **Russian Switzerland (Russkaya Shveytsariya)** *at the same time, were you not?*

I began *Izmail* in Russia, but when I came to Switzerland I stopped, because when you come to another milieu, you have to adapt, and you start changing very rapidly. You suddenly discover things in yourself that were always there, but they weren't needed. It's important for a writer, the same as for any person, to change in general, but it's especially important to be able to change quickly in order to produce new works. If you don't change, you'll be writing the same novel your entire life. To write a different novel, you yourself have to change. It helps to go to another country, where you have to change much more rapidly than you did at home, but while you are still changing, you have to stop writing your novel. So I stopped and I began to change. Changing also means learning something. And in order to change more quickly I had to write *Russian Switzerland*. I had to understand who I was and where and what sort of connections I had. Why did Karamzin stop writing prose and start writing Russian history? Because you can't live without a floor, soil, ground beneath your feet. There was no history, so he had to write the history of his country in order to understand what had been before him, where and who he was. It was the same with me — when I found myself in a vacuum in Switzerland, I began writing my own

Russian history. I produced a history of Russians, but through Russians who had been to Switzerland. When I had written this book, *Izmail* followed immediately. I finished *Russian Switzerland* and *Izmail* almost simultaneously. *Russian Switzerland*, however, is basically a book of quotations. I had to read a great deal and collect everything that Russians had written about Switzerland. The result was a book about Russia, which was written not by me but by the Russians themselves. In the end I became a compiler of Russian history.

In your second book of essays In the Footsteps of Byron and Tolstoy (Auf den Spuren von Byron und Tolstoj) *there is also much about Russia.*

Actually, this happens to be a book not about Russia. *Russian Switzerland* is entirely about Russia from the perspective of Russians and Switzerland. That is why it reads so well in Russian and looks odd in translation, where it is simply a collection of cultural and historical information. In Russian, on the other hand, it is like an incredibly vibrant living organism, because it is not simply a collection of texts, it consists cover to cover of impassioned commentaries on issues that are still relevant and always will be. In translation, however, the civic fervor of this burning question "Whither Russia?" disappears, and all that remains is "who slept where and when, what they said, ate," etc.

In the Footsteps of Byron and Tolstoy I was no longer interested in Russia but wanted to understand non-Russia. I had stepped outside the boundaries of the Russian world, as it were, and it proved to be impossible to understand this other world in Russian. Yes, the language creates meaning. So I had to switch to German. I wrote the book for readers who share with me the experience of life outside Russia.

It is of course about neither Russia nor Switzerland. Or rather, it is about both Russia and Switzerland, but what it is really about is how creative individuals relate to death. What did they have in common? Byron was twenty-eight, and Tolstoy was twenty-eight. They were in the same situation as anyone who writes and they confronted the same problem, namely, what to do in this life, since you are going to die. So you prepare for death your entire life, and your entire life you try to fight death with your pen and your words. This is what the book is about. Actually, the title of the book is *Montreux – Missolunghi – Astapovo*. In my mind and theirs throughout was the end point: "Where do their travels take them?" Montreux is where we started, Missolunghi is the place in Greece where Byron died, and Astapovo is the railroad station in Russia where Tolstoy died.

Yes, but that's a long way off — that's Russia, that's death.

Actually, the most important thing for me is where they are going. Their walk through the Alps becomes a metaphorical stroll through eternity. And the point is how to enter eternity and take this world with you. Tolstoy worked on this question his whole life, and it's interesting for me to understand what happened to him and how.

In the end Tolstoy becomes the main character, and he seems quite close to you.

Absolutely. All nineteenth-century writers are dear to me, and I love them all — good and bad. In this sense Nabokov played a wicked joke on Russian literature by dividing all authors into "black" and "white." After him, Chernyshevsky, let's say, is a bad writer — you aren't supposed to read him, you're not supposed to praise him. As for me, I love the old

Russian literature of the nineteenth century, from which the twentieth gets all its vital juices. I always compare it to love of a woman, because if you love a woman, you love all of her, all parts of her. You can't just love one part and not love some other one. So I love Chernyshevsky just as much as I do Tolstoy. Nevertheless, there are writers that you do or do not identify with. Nabokov, for example, is one of my favorites, so he and I generally coincide purely stylistically. He worshipped Tolstoy and hated Dostoyevsky. I love them all, but I can read Tolstoy all the time and anywhere. And as I was writing my book it was such a pleasure to be able to once again just take any book of Tolstoy's and open it. As Nabokov put it in his lecture on *Anna Karenina*: "When you read Turgenev, you know that you are reading Turgenev; when you read Tolstoy, you read because you cannot stop." It's the same thing with me. I mean, when I read Dostoyevsky, I know that I am reading a novel, and quite frankly, there aren't many works of his that I can read more than a few pages of, because his disregard for language irritates me tremendously.

Your novels and your non-fiction share one stylistic feature, namely the frequent use of both verbal and stylistic quotations. Why is it important for you to include quotations in your texts?

Well, I wasn't born into this world in a wasteland. There was a huge body of culture here before me, and all the words that have been spoken have already become human. Each word and each phrase uttered so many times before me is full of love, and hate, and fear. It would be very naïve and stupid of me not to take this into account — and arrogant. Because all words have already been uttered by someone, I have to be careful to use them all, and when I use them I am integrating all culture before me into my texts. It is very important to me to feel tradition and to feel myself a part of tradition — a little link in the infinite chain that was there before me and, I hope, will be there when I am gone. Thus every quotation goes into the solid foundation of the pyramid I am building. I know that I am only putting a little brick at the top of this gigantic pyramid of all literature that has come before me. I think that the development of literature is a progressive process, and that the only way I can say something new is to use everything that has been said before me. Since I do so consciously, it is not even a device but a principle. And I try to make each work a total text that absorbs all previous culture and literature.

The style of your novels is quite personal and difficult to describe. One could say that they are collections of texts, large chunks of diverse types of prose that flow together to form an entirely original mosaic.

But that is my goal! That is the technical aim I set myself — to absorb everything that has existed before me; that is, ideally there should be a kind of ideal text. The composition — the mosaic picture that I create out of these individual stones — must be my own picture. I bear responsibility for the picture that results, for the image or face that appears on the mosaic when I have inserted the last stone into it.

And an entirely new dynamic is created in this picture.

Every style is made up of energy, the age, personality. When I select particular bits of energy from different ages or styles and combine them, a third effect is produced: energy multiplied by another energy becomes a kind of nuclear energy. This energy, this power is not contained in these phrases taken individually, but combined they generate an amazing nuclear effect.

In the section from the diary of an early twentieth-century young Russian gentlewoman in Hair of Venus *there is an extensive and almost verbatim quotation from the memoirs of the writer Vera Panova. You do not mention this fact anywhere, however, and you have been accused of plagiarism. What is your reaction to that?*

Well, I'm sorry that people don't understand what I'm doing, and that they haven't actually read my works. Because besides Vera Panova I quote five hundred, if not thousands, of other writers, male and female, and pages and pages are full of quotations! This is all part of the harassment against me, you see, because *Novy mir* and *Literaturnaya gazeta* are always after me. They carry the most awful, vile, dirty articles about me and my texts. Someone there sights a quotation from one author but doesn't notice quotations from five hundred others, and then writes that this is plagiarism. The whole notion of plagiarism seems ridiculous to me, since after Bakhtin[1] we all live in someone else's words. So no comment.

You're not troubled then...

Since people haven't read the novel but have read that article, it means that Shishkin stole the novel from Vera Panova. In that case I have to say that the work in question by Vera Panova is not her fiction but her reminiscences of childhood and school in Rostov. She attended the same secondary school as my heroine Izabella Yurieva. They had the same house porter and bought pens from the same clerk in Iosif Pokorny's shop, and it was just such ribbons that they both tied to their albums as little girls. I thought it was important

[1]Mikhail Bakhtin (1895-1975), Russian literary theorist whose wide-ranging ideas significantly influenced the Russian and Western thinking in cultural history, linguistics, literary theory, and aesthetics.

to reproduce real-life details in exactly the same form, and so I went looking in thousands of books for all of these minutiae from Rostov and the life of that student.

These days most writers write on the computer, and so do you. In **In the Footsteps of Byron and Tolstoy** *your computer is your most faithful companion. Would the book have turned out differently without it?*

I don't think that the book would have turned out at all without the computer. Literature, of course, is not a technical form of art, like, say the cinema. Obviously, the cinema is going to develop much faster technologically, because every ten or fifteen years new technologies come along that immediately affect photography and the art of the motion picture. You could say that technology is what makes the cinema. Technology does not make literature, but it does have an impact. Novels written longhand will never resemble texts written on a computer. In that sense, first of all, the computer has in fact become the hero of my novel, and in the second, it was simultaneously both creator and creation.

Probably a quotation depository as well?

Indeed, in that sense it was the creator of my text — a co-creator in any case.

So you store quotations in the computer and not in your memory?

I can't keep anything in my memory. In this sense the computer is a kind of image of the creative method we discussed earlier, where everything written before you suddenly shows up in your work. You can't do that in your head. It's possible with the computer, inasmuch as the computer becomes your hand, as it were, a part of you, a part of your head, a kind of parallel brain. So suddenly it turns out that in your head you have quotations from everything written before you and can immediately use them any time you want.

Some people in Russia are surprised that you are working productively abroad. They say that you have supposedly "been robbed of your native language." This doesn't seem to be a problem for you, or is it?

I think and talk about this constantly, and everyone asks me this question. I already know the correct answer. First of all, it wasn't Russian writers who came up with the idea that a Russian writer cannot write outside Russia, but Russian rulers, who lost control of writers living abroad. It is a myth invented by tyrants.

The second question is in fact important. What should you do if you lose touch with the living language, which changes very rapidly? Two things: one is to hitch up your pants and go running after all the changes in the language, which is changing so quickly that you're not going to catch up anyway, even if you live in Russia. Because any novel written today uses slang and advertising. Take Pelevin, for example. I'm not saying it's good or bad; I just want to say that tomorrow this sort of text will no longer be readable, because the world on which it is based — the world of today's quotations, slang, and advertisements — will have disappeared. This solution is no good for me in any case — I wouldn't have it in Russia either — and I'm not interested in chasing after a "today" that is going to disappear tomorrow. I need to say more important things that will be relevant tomorrow, and the day after tomorrow, and forever. For that reason I have to take another path — the opposite one — by creating a language of my own that will exist outside of time. Where you work on this language — in Russia or in Switzerland — is not important. I'd work on it if I lived in Antarctica.

Now you have begun to write in German as well, but that must be something quite different. Is it perhaps a second love of yours?

I'm not out after the laurels of Nabokov or Conrad, who switched from their native languages to English. I'm perfectly aware that although I have a certain level of proficiency, my German has limits beyond which my feel for the language cannot go. I will never write fiction in German, because you have to write fiction incorrectly and sense the incorrectness, and I can play with incorrectness only in Russian. German I can only write correctly — only nonfiction can be written correctly. In other words, if I want to convey information, I can do so in German, but when the language itself is the information, I can write only in Russian.

Would you in principle be interested in translating literary fiction from German to Russian?

No! No, for a number of reasons. For one thing, I can't read German writers, because I don't think what they are doing is very interesting. In other words, there is no German writer I'd want to read in Russian in the first place. And second, I've already had some experience in translating — I began translating a German short story into Russian when I was still quite young. But in the end I started improving the story by rewriting it: changing the plot, adding an ending! The story was undoubtedly improved, but this is not literary translation. And that's why I don't intend ever to do any such translation.

The notion "universal harmony" often appears in your texts, and you have even remarked that this is what your novels are ultimately about. What do you mean by that?

What I mean here is God, of course. When you look at icons and medieval art you can see that people back then lived in a world of universal harmony, even if some icons portray all sorts of horrors. If God exists, however, everything is not so horrible, everything has meaning, and we will all reach our historical motherland, where we are loved and expected. This is what I mean by universal harmony. And vice versa — when I read a text that lacks this ultimate, divine, final warmth and I sense that the author does not love his heroes, I feel that I myself am deserted and abandoned and without God, for I identify with the hero. The author is in a way God to his hero, and if God doesn't love his hero, then He doesn't love me either, if He exists at all. But when a picture or literary or musical work has this feeling of final, ultimate warmth, then no matter how frightening things may be now, no matter what horrors take place in this world — concentration camps, wars, terrorists... if in the final analysis we are all moving toward this historical homeland where each of us is loved and expected, then life would seem to be worth living.

Vladimir SOROKIN

Renate von Mangoldt

"We have cosmic goals, not just comfort and reproduction. We are not meat machines."

Vladimir Georgievich Sorokin was born on 7 August 1955 in the town of Bykovo near Moscow. In 1977 he graduated from the Gubkin Institute of Oil and Gas in Moscow with a degree in mechanical engineering. He worked at the *Smena* magazine for a while but was fired for refusing to join the Komsomol. He made a living as a book designer and also devoted himself to painting and conceptual art. He developed as an author among the artists and writers of the Moscow underground in the 1980s.

In 1985 a selection of six stories appeared in the Paris journal *A-Ya,* and *Sintaksis* in France published *The Queue* (*Ochered*). In Russia *The Queue* appeared in 1992 in the journal *Iskusstvo kino*, and a collection of short stories published in Moscow was short-listed for the Russian Booker Prize, as was the manuscript of his novel *Four Stout Hearts* (*Serdtsa chetyrekh*). Sorokin's works have been published in the West by prominent houses such as Gallimard, Fischer, DuMont, BV Berlin, and Verlag der Autoren and have been translated into several languages, including Japanese and Korean. In 2001 he was awarded the Andrey Bely

Prize "for outstanding contribution to Russian literature." In 2005 he received the German Ministry of Culture Liberty prize. He is a member of the Russian PEN Club.

Sorokin was persecuted by the conservative youth action group "Moving Together" ("Idushchie vmeste") and taken to court for pornography in connection with his 1999 novel *Blue Lard* (*Goluboe salo*).

2002 through 2005 saw the publication of a trilogy consisting of the novels *Ice* (*Led*), *Bro's Way* (*Put Bro*), and *2300*. His anti-utopian tale *The Day of the Oprichnik* (*Den oprichnika*) appeared in 2006. He has also written a number of film scripts, and in 2005 he was commissioned by the Bolshoi Theater to write the libretto to Leonid Desyatnikov's opera *Rosenthal's Children* (*Deti Rozentalya*).

Let's begin by talking about your early prose. In retrospect it's even difficult to understand how you could work so single-mindedly, beginning with the short stories and the novel **The Queue (Ochered)**. *What was the stimulus — some sort of moral duty to make sense of the society in which you lived, perhaps, or the need for self-understanding? Or did you just find it interesting?*

I think it was all of that together. It was the desire to make sense of the society in which we found ourselves — a fantastic society, a mythological state. It was also the desire to make sense of myself. Literature, after all, is a mechanism of self-understanding. And it was pleasure. This process gives me as much pleasure as love. So everything together.

It might be said that you have moved ahead through a complete program of deconstruction. If **The Norm (Norma)** *deconstructs Soviet mythology,* **A Novel (Roman)** *decon-structs the Russian novel, and* **Marina's Thirtieth Love (Tridtsataya lyubov Mariny)** *is a deconstruction of Socialist Realism. But as you see it today, is there anything in these novels besides a powerful attack on the totalitarian world?*

Marina's Thirtieth Love was planned as a binary bomb consisting of two parts. The first part shows grotesque Moscow life, and in the second the heroine dissolves in the official Soviet language and ideology. She loses her own personality and is depersonalized. I wrote it more than twenty years ago. Then everyone read only the first part and leafed through the second, because obviously, they all lived in this language. But now it's the other way around. Everyone reads through the second part with great interest, because now this language is utterly dead. It is the language of a deceased mythological empire. It reads like fossilized literature, something that has been dug up out of the ground. Time does that, and something similar happens to many texts. If some of my stories were earlier taken to be the purest Sotsart, today they read like strict Realism.

Documentary literature?

Yes, this is proof that literature truly is read in different ways. Tolstoy is read in various ways, as is Dostoyevsky, depending on when they are read. In other words, we change, the world changes, and literature that has already been written changes along with us.

You have an unusual talent for imitation, and what you do with stereotypes seems like a documentary description of the Soviet Union. Today **The Queue** *probably reads like a reconstruction of Soviet life and the Russian language of the period.*

As a de-construction or a re-construction?

A re-construction.

Yes. I've thought of writing *The Queue 2*. There are lines now as well but they are for different things. For example, there is a line in the airport when you go through security control. I've seen enormous lines, very long ones. They are entirely different, in a way, but people in them talk the same.

Yet the language has changed.

The language has changed, but not the mentality. After all, a mere 25 years have passed since I wrote *The Queue*. Can the mentality of a nation change in 25 years?

Still, now in the Russian state there have been such enormous changes that surely on some level they affect both the mentality and the language. Everyday life, quite simply.

Yes, formally the changes have been great, but people are not reading *The Queue* as retro-literature or as an artifact of the period. Take away the Soviet realia, and the episode with the woman who saves a man from the line could take place anywhere — in China, or even in Sweden. I don't know whether you have lines or what they are for.

We have the same lines at the airport. Your other early novels cannot be read like that. Obviously, you don't want to say literally that Soviet citizens regularly eat shit, but there are episodes there that could make readers gag, even if they understand and are sympathetic toward the way you work.

The thing is that then I was writing so-called "cruel" literature. Once at a reading in Israel someone stood up and said something that was right on the mark. There were questions about why I was writing things in the '80s that shocked people and made them want to vomit. I tried to explain, but of course an author can't really explain anything properly. But this person said it very well: in that country it was the only writing that was moving forward to broaden literary space; it was a jolt that expanded reality. I think that I was simply clearing myself a place for a new aesthetics. And works like *Ice* took shape on this new cleared space. But I had to live to the age of fifty to understand why I was doing all this.

Readers reacted very strongly emotionally. Do you think that such reactions helped or hindered the reading of your texts?

I think that my works were meant to create shock, it is a component built into the project itself, not something secondary.

I remember the reaction of some critics. You were accused of many things, including that you were writing for Western Slavists...

Meaning for you?

...that the most important thing for you was commercial success, and that you are betraying Russian literature, discrediting the very concept of Russian prose. Do you remember?

These were not the harshest statements. Others said that if Sorokin is sick, he needs treatment.

And if he's healthy, he should be put on trial.

There is more in my works than just "shock therapy," however. People who react unhealthily to this shock are in my opinion not particularly smart. Especially the critics who can't find anything else.

You're not offended?

Well, perhaps if it were some Western Slavist saying all this… But these are people who cannot approach literature as literature. As before, they think of it as something sacred. There is a kind of secret in literature and the literary process, to be sure. But literature is not a temple, and it should not be assigned the function of sacred texts. Literature is written by lay people. Russian writers shouldn't be made into priests. Saints and ascetics did not concern themselves with literature. They lived in cells, prayed, and were concerned with spiritual training. But we are concerned with literature. It's a kind of experiment, a secular occupation, like building a table, for instance.

An area where aesthetics would seem to precede ethics.

To me literature is not "what" but rather "how." It's what gives us aesthetic pleasure. I realize that sometimes mathematics can also give aesthetic pleasure, but not everyone understands the language of formulas, while to this day we can't live without literature.

You've said somewhere that you are a Romantic. In what sense?

I believe that humanity is not yet perfect, but that it will be perfected, that contemporary humans are thus far imperfect beings, that we still do not know ourselves or our potential, that we have not understood that we are cosmic beings.

We are created by a higher intelligence, and we have cosmic goals, not just comfort and reproduction. We are not "meat machines." So on this issue I am a Romantic.

I read your article in **Ex Libris** *in which you say that by and large there is only one theme, one fateful question that confounds you, namely "What is violence?"*

Yes, this is a mystery. Why can't people do without

violence? Why can't they keep from killing? This is a mystery to me, and I try to talk about it in literary form.

In your early works you immerse the reader in a constant state of moral chaos full of killing and torture for no obvious reason. But you also have written more than once about violence on a grand scale -- Communism and Nazism. On a grand scale there is an idea, a lofty goal. There, as in **Four Stout Hearts**, *and* **Ice**, *and* **Bro's Way** *the killing takes place in the name of a lofty goal.*

The entire history of the twentieth century is the history of total violence — violence based on ideology. It is even more terrible when the state is the killer. When a person stabs someone to death it is murder, but when the state forces some people to kill others, it is double murder. For the state kills not only the victims, but also the souls of the people doing the killing. Why am I against capital punishment? No one stops to think about the fact that there is such a thing as the office of executioner. When the state says: "kill, I permit you to kill," it makes him a legalized murderer. After all, the state cannot resurrect a man, so there is a double absurdity here. There is one victim, and then one more is added. The machine of the state multiplies the murder. This huge theme of violence, unfortunately, is inexhaustible.

This theme is also connected with Germany.

Not only — why do you say that? With both the Soviet Union and Fascist Germany. In the latter half of the '80s I became actively interested in totalitarian practices, both Soviet and non-Soviet. I wrote several works having to do with German totalitarianism — "*A Month in Dachau*"(*Mesyats v Dakhau*), for example.

And **Blue Lard.**

Blue Lard and the play **Hochzeitsreise.**
Is there a notable difference, in your opinion?

The difference is purely formal. The chief architects of totalitarianism, Hitler and Stalin, treated humans similarly — as matter, as things. They were both atheists and both grasped for power, but there were also differences. Hitler didn't understand why Stalin was destroying his own elite, and Stalin didn't understand why Hitler held to his racial theory. Hitler had the idea of blood — "Blut und Boden," and Stalin had the concept of the socialist state and equality. But they shared the same principle, which was to treat the individual as simply part of the masses. This is typical of the twentieth century in general. Brodsky wrote, "A tree is dearer to me than the forest." But for them it was the other way around. The people were more important to them than any individual human being. The strangest thing that happened in the twentieth century was that the individual lost his or her personal biography and dissolved into the biography of the masses. This is what generated mass art, mass taste, and so on.

The content of **Ice** *is not so simple. There we meet a sect of people who are searching for a tree in the forest in order to communicate with each other.*

A tree that speaks with its heart...

... and that at the same time ruthlessly kills others.

To my mind the entire *Ice Trilogy* is a discussion of the twentieth century. It's a kind of monument to it. You can look at this as a metaphor, or as science fiction, or as some sort of conspiratorial novel, although I consider it a metaphor more than anything else, an attempt to generalize. Only now have I begun to realize and reflect on the matter. I worked on the trilogy for five years, and now I'm beginning to look at it as a reader. Basically, it's the idea of selection. Any totalitarian practice, after all — beginning with the state and ending with totalitarian sects — is based on selection, a division of the world into "us and them." That is, our people and the other.

Because they are all striving toward spiritual paradise, the blue-eyed, blond "children of light" seem to recall the cruel heroes of **Four Stout Hearts.** *Do you see anything specifically Russian in these existential quests?*

No doubt. Russians are certainly not the only ones who long for paradise on earth, but there is a great deal of Russianness there, including the notion of self-sacrifice for a lofty idea on which the Russian Revolution depended. Before this novel was written the Tungus meteorite generated a lot of myths. There was a society that organized annual expeditions to the site. People are waiting for a miracle. Something fell out of the sky, something mysterious that was never found.

How did you hit on the idea of the **Ice** *trilogy?*

I didn't know anything when I began writing it. The idea came to me in Japan, where I was teaching Russian language and literature. It was a very hot July, and that was how I started thinking about ice. When I had written the novel, however, I was sure that it was already finished and that as usual I would wait for it to come out and begin writing something else. But it wouldn't let me go, and for a year I couldn't write anything new. I had some good ideas for novels and I'd begin to write, but they didn't take off. And so I returned to *Ice*. I realized that I had touched upon the theme, but that it wasn't finished. And some intelligent people told me the same thing — they wanted more. Most important, I wanted more. So after this came the first part of *Bro's Way*.

The novel that begins "I was born in 1908..."

That was the year the Tungus meteorite fell. Now the three parts are there, and I hope that this story will finally let me go.

At some point you said that **Ice** *is your disappointed reaction to today's intelligentsia.*

Not only the intelligentsia but also contemporary civilization in general. The intelligentsia is not the worst part. More precisely, contemporary civilization means the entire twentieth century, whose ready-made goods for mass consumption, mediocre taste and mass production have gradually transformed people into "meat machines." Multiply this by the total atheism advancing upon us, and human beings become a cog in this machine and lose their cosmism and divine image. To me this truly is one form of disappointment. It's frightening that all cities are beginning to resemble each other, and although they speak different languages, people are becoming the same and dressing the same. The complete unification of humanity is under way. The average person on whom totalitarian regimes depends has triumphed. These are people with mediocre potential and mediocre demands. My trilogy is about this as well, of course.

In that case it presents a panorama of the twentieth century, and not just Russia.

The final part does, yes. It's about people of various nationalities, and very little of it takes place in Russia.

Does Socialist Realism live on in contemporary literature?

Socialist Realism grew out of classical Russian literature. Take Turgenev's *Fathers and Sons*, for example — many motifs there resemble the method of Socialist Realism. I'm not speaking about Chernyshevsky, who was one of the founders of Socialist Realism. There is quite a bit of Socialist Realism in certain contemporary detective novels — features that show through. As a method, however, it has not survived its time, but perished along with the Soviet Union. I've written about this in an anthology that contains one paragraph on Socialist Realism. I don't think the name is accurate, because it does not express the method in its entirety. Sinyavsky tried to write about this. You remember, Socialist Realism as Classicism. In reality it's eclectic, and grew out of two or three novels — Gorky, Chernyshevsky...

Brodsky would also name Tolstoy.

Resurrection, of course. They borrowed Tolstoy's didacticism. But in fact all of that has died.

You must have read How the Steel was Tempered (Kak zakalyalas stal) at school. Do you remember your reaction?

I began reading the Russian classics when I was quite young. I read *Dead Souls* when I was thirteen and Dostoevsky also early on, and I soon understood what good literature was. Ostrovsky's novel is trash — not literature at all, but a kind of hagiography of a Soviet saint. You have the vitae of St. Mary of Egypt and St. Anthony, and this hero is a Soviet saint who lies paralyzed and tells us how to live, and that we ought to give our entire lives to the state. His image itself is very gloomy. In reality this is a necrophilic novel. Interestingly enough, the novel contains several scenes of attempted rape, most of which are unsuccessful. I think the author must have had serious complexes, but the book is certainly bad and has not survived the Soviet Union. To my mind the chief criterion of any literature is its convertibility. If the currency of a given country is not convertible, it means that it is weak. If Tolstoy is convertible and his books can be found in any Western bookstore, it means he is a good writer. And if Nikolai Ostrovsky is unknown in Sweden, it simply means that he is a bad writer.

That argument is a little risky. As you know, Pushkin is not very well known abroad. But how do you explain the success of the film **The Matrix** *among the Russian intelligentsia?*

It's an interesting film, at any rate. It's popular and in fact does formulate a problem. I'm not speaking about the form — it's a blockbuster — but its idea is rather profound. What it is about is again the fact that the world is changing and that our civilization has so conquered our consciousness that we are beginning to lose certain innate abilities. For example, we can refuse to believe that this piano here is not some kind of computerized projection. All of this makes me sad.

Several times already you have talked about unification as a process going on in society. Is that perhaps why you are so interested in cloning?

Yes, and I do not believe in human engineering. The idea that people want to create people and be creators is dangerous and can lead us into a dead end, but it's a very challenging notion in literature. Through cloning you can show contemporary humans, the state of their minds, what they want. It comes from dissatisfaction with themselves, because otherwise they would not want to be cloned.

Or the other way round.

That also comes from a mass-consumer society. More and more forms have to be created to assure constant choice. Go into a modern supermarket and you'll see one hundred kinds of sausage. To me that is a symbol of the twentieth century: one hundred kinds of sausage, and one idea.

In your latest novel **The Day of the Oprichnik,** *there is something I think is entirely new in Russian literature, namely the idea of describing the horrible reign of Ivan the Terrible and connecting it with the future of Russia. How did you decide upon such a choice?*

Paradoxically, *Oprichnina* as such has so far hardly been described at all in Russian literature. There is only A. K. Tolstoy's *Prince Serebryany*, and even that novel merely touches upon the theme. For fully understandable reasons, none of our classics has ventured to tackle this awful subject, because no description of the pathological bloody deeds of the sixteenth-century *oprichniki* in the language of nineteenth-century Russian realism would ever have made it past the censor. In my opinion, any phenomenon in Russian history that has not yet been described in literature is still *alive*. And the idea of the *Oprichnina* — servants of the state who stand *apart* from it and to whom all is permitted — lives on in the Russian mentality to the present day.

In *Day of the Oprichnik* I model the situation toward which I think contemporary Russia is moving — self-isolation, immersion in her past, a view of the European world as hostile. By 2028 a Great Wall of Russia will be built, behind which there will be a New Russia whose past has become her future. In such a situation the State will not be able to get along without its faithful hounds. And Russians can become *oprichniki* very easily. It suffices to revive in the popular memory the archetype of the state servant who stands *apart* and has absolute authority. Basically, there is a little of the *oprichnik* in every Russian official. In my book the *oprichniki* are born again in the twenty-first century.

Tatyana TOLSTAYA

N. Kochnev

"The intellectual by definition is someone who is aware of things, at least, whereas the people are those who are not aware of anything."

Tatyana Nikitichna Tolstaya was born on 3 May 1951 in Leningrad into the large family of Professor of Physics Nikita Tolstoy, son of the famous writer Alexei Tolstoy. Her maternal grandfather was the renowned translator Mikhail Lozinsky.

After graduating from the Department of Classical Philology at Leningrad State University in 1974, she moved to Moscow, where until 1983 she worked at the Department of Oriental Literature at the Nauka publishing house.

Tolstaya's first short story *On the Golden Porch (Na zolotom kryltse sideli..)* appeared in the *Avrora* magazine in 1983. In 1987 she published her first collection of stories under the same title.

In 1990 she went to the United States to teach Russian literature, and over the next ten years she spent several months a year there. In 1991 she wrote the column *My Belfry (Svoya kolokolnya)* for the weekly *Moscow News* and was on the editorial board of the *Stolitsa* magazine.

Her works have been translated into English, German,

French, and several other languages. In 2000, after the publication of her novel *The Slynx* (*Kys*), she received the Triumph Prize for literary achievement. Tolstaya currently hosts the television talk show *Shkola zlosloviya* (*School of Slander*).

You are the granddaughter of Aleksei Tolstoy and the prominent translator Mikhail Lozinsky. What attitude toward literature did you inherit from them?

The thing is that when I read Aleksei Tolstoy — and I did read him — I read him, whereas when I read works translated by Lozinsky I wasn't reading him, but the writers he translated, and it didn't interest me very much. It was mainly poetry, and as a young child you don't like poetry — it's too difficult. You begin to appreciate it when you reach a certain age, and then your attitude is quite different. I mean, they are completely different things. In general the reason you start writing is not because you've read someone. It's something genetic. But it's hard to say whose genes I have more of.

What writers were important in your home?

We didn't discuss literature. My father was an extra-ordinarily well-educated man, educated in all respects: he was a physicist and a scholar, but he was also well educated in the literary sense. He read everything, knew three languages, and he was interested in everything in the humanities — literature, and poetry, and music, and art, and psychology, and philosophy. So we talked about everything in general, but about literature least of all. We read various books and took a great deal from books, and we had our own ideas about things. We had our own tastes. We very seldom discussed any specific literary works. My parents, quite simply, and especially my father, set an example of respect for all work and all kinds of creativity. And the atmosphere at home was unconstrained — partly the way we were brought up, and something genetically inherent in all of us — the lack of envy toward anybody, the ability to be happy for someone else's achievements. I never saw any trace of envy in our family.

So no one at home educated you in literature?

No one did anything. The house was full of books, quite simply.

Was it easy or difficult for you to begin writing as a member of this family?

I was thirty-two when I began writing. Before that I hadn't written anything. Well, there were some things we wrote for each other at home — poems for birthdays and New Year's, we put on plays... But all that was strictly for home, and no one wanted to take it in front of an audience. And the moment I began writing it was all the same to me; that is, it just happened to me one fine day, and it was all the same — family or no family, name or no name. I was just very sure of myself, and without this confidence I wouldn't have begun to come out in the open.

But you already had a certain background or frame-work or standards within which to work.

I understand what you're saying, but I'm not sure I took all that into account. We all work within a certain framework. I know very well what I like and what I don't like. I make my own framework. Take Aleksei Tolstoy. Turgenev was his favorite writer, and when he began to write he deliberately tried to imitate Turgenev; that is, in a way he became Turgenev. He thought that everyone would notice, that it would be terrible, that everyone would see that he was writing like Turgenev. No one ever noticed anything, however, because what he wrote wasn't like Turgenev. I mean, in order to write he had to imagine he was Turgenev. I don't like Turgenev at all. There's nothing there for me, you understand.

Thirty-two, you said. Where were you living then — in Leningrad or in Moscow already?

In Moscow. But Leningrad or Moscow — it made no difference. Nothing interesting was published in those years. There wasn't anything to read — only old books. As for contemporary literature, everything was suppressed by the censorship. There was practically nothing to read. Very rarely. There were Trifonov's novels — that was the early seventies. Yes, I like Trifonov a lot. But only some of him, and only in the seventies. Otherwise there was nothing. I read the literary journals the whole time, but it was terrible, simply terrible. Nothing was right; everything made you want to protest: that's not the way to write, those aren't the right words, that's not the right syntax, you don't have to make it so long. I disliked everything.

I remember very well when your stories appeared in the eighties. They were like a fresh wind from the east. You were quickly translated into many languages, but it seems that in Russia you weren't published readily.

It wasn't quite like that. I began publishing in 1983, and in 1983 the better you wrote, the harder it was to get published. That is, since they wouldn't let you get into print, you could consider that to be your reward — the fact that they wouldn't do it for anything. These were insurmountable difficulties, because everything was controlled by the bosses, the censorship; for the people at the top the main thing is control, keeping everything under control, making sure everything is gray, smooth, the same. Overall the Soviet system was such that everyone was supposed to be the same, a uniform gray. Then it's safe; then there isn't any colorful individuality. If someone showed any individuality it meant that he was out of control, and he had to be brought under control; no one was supposed to arouse any emotions, thoughts, feelings — if they did they had to be removed from literature. So it was extremely difficult to get into literature. In 1983 something stirred just a little, and then later, of course, everything was fine.

You had good timing.

Yes, my timing was good, because otherwise I don't know what would have happened. Well, of course, there are new people who are free, and old people used to the old system. I heard only bad things from the old ones. From the new ones I heard either good things or various, so to speak. But from these old Soviet people I heard nothing but anger. And then, of course, there are people who would like to do what you're doing but can't — they complain and become upset. I've run into this kind of very cheap envy a number of times.

Because the critics liked you?

There are critics and critics. We don't have any good ones. Many of them criticize, but they are not interesting. We have almost no literary criticism. What we have is newspaper criticism.

What about newspaper critics in the West?

There are all kinds. Slavists, of course, write philological criticism. As for the newspaper people... well, they seem to work according to some sort of principles of their own. For a long time here — in the early nineties, for example — newspaper criticism was not in fact criticism at all. That is, the main thing for critics was to show off their mastery of the language and to make sure no one could understand anything. In other words, it was their own little project. Very few of them actually read your text conscientiously and responsibly and tried to convey to the reader their sense of the text, few have a value system of their own according to which they are judging it. There's none of that. What we have are private performances and conversations, but no culture of criticism. And today almost nothing remains of it — there are literally one or two critics worthy of the name who think about literature and readers rather than just themselves.

Then the situation changed. Now you are constantly being asked for new works. Is that a nuisance or perhaps even a burden to you?

Everyone is always demanding something from me. Well, not any more, but earlier they were endlessly asking for new texts. It's useless to demand anything from me, because I have no intention whatever of playing by the rules established for themselves by the other writers. And who has the right to demand a text from me – do they want me to hurry up with the birth process?!

Was this a bother or did you ignore it?

I'm capable of ignoring absolutely anything. All of these so-called literary situations that crop up all around really don't concern me at all. I don't intend to hurry, or do what I'm expected to do, or publish a book a year, or begin writing novels, or stop writing novels, until I'm ready. I'm not going to do anything I don't want to do. I'm only going to do what I want and can, because I feel responsible to someone or something inside me and not at all to readers, the public, or the critics. Nor should I, in my opinion.

You were born and grew up in a city famous for its literature. Is it possible to regard the stylistic sophistication of your stories as examples of the Petersburg literary tradition?

Tradition or no tradition… I think that the writer can't know this and shouldn't — it should be something visible from outside. When you yourself are writing, you don't exist in any tradition: you write and try as best you can to get this jigsaw puzzle to hang together. It will never fit together perfectly, but you try to make as few mistakes as possible. This is a purely internal problem for you alone, and you can't correspond or not correspond to any particular tradition.

Now there are other writers — mostly avant-garde writers — who invent for themselves some other system of writing and follow it. In other words, they don't write from within, but play with Lego bricks. They have their rules, they have their manifestoes, they have a tradition. They are very careful either to fit into a given tradition or, on the contrary, to go against it in order to do something no one has ever done before. Well, it's an experiment. And this experiment is their problem. But this isn't genuine writing — it's just another game.

You, of course, work in a different way. Perhaps that is why your stories seem to exist outside of time. Sometimes it even seems that they could have been written before the Revolution. How do you view your early prose?

I'm fine with just about all of it. There's very little that I don't like and would want to rewrite. But I never rewrite; I never return: what's done is done. I don't like to redo anything.

Where did you get the idea for **The Slynx** *and how did you decide to take on such an amazingly complex project?*

I started it in 1986. Not long before that I had begun writing some things and realized that what I was doing were not short stories as before, but longer stories. I simply began writing a short story, but then I saw that for some reason it wasn't working out, because I had to say this and that and explain this and that. That is, I noticed that I was writing a novel — not a novella and not a long story, but a novel. If you begin writing something and you write an exposition or a first scene, you can generally imagine how many pages it will take to make the thing turn out properly — you'll see this, because it's a different tempo. Yes — there is a definite tempo of some sort. And I realized that if I continued, it would become a novel. But I still didn't know how to write it.

So the beginning was the same as in your novel: "Benedict pulled on his felt boots..."

Yes, that's how it began. But to describe it — there's a definite tempo, an unhurried tempo. So you think to yourself something like "aha, here there should be so many characters and so many scenes, and you have to embrace this part of life, and this part of life, and that part of life. You have to describe this, you have to explain that. So there you have at least two or three hundred pages, even though I try to write as compactly as possible. I don't like to drag things out, but some things demand detailed description. So I had to write a novel, but I wasn't ready; I didn't know how to do it. "Well, let's see," I thought. So I wrote on and in the process I studied how to write a novel; that is, I heard some sort of entirely different inner voices. And it took many years, because sometimes I had to put it aside and think. Sometimes nothing worked for a year or a year and a half. I didn't have a chance to write, quite simply. I was living in the United States, and there I had to get organized somehow, make a living, teach, write articles for American journals. That's something completely, completely different! And there was an unpleasant side to it — you write something in Russian, and it's all lost in translation. So why try to write in Russian — and I can't help trying — but you write, and your words disappear.

Back to the novel. There is an opinion that **The Slynx** *has nothing in common with your prose of the 1980s. Do you agree?*

Yes, I think I do.

To me it seems that it has something in common nevertheless. For example, one senses a deep sadness both in your stories and in **The Slynx** *for what has been lost in Russia.*

In that sense, yes, absolutely. That is, in terms of the language there's little in common, but in terms of the idea, of course there is.

With respect to the language, it seems to me that although the context is entirely different you use certain linguistic features both in the early stories and in the novel — literary quotations and associations, for example.

Well, yes, although much less in the stories, whereas here it is a regular device. And then, if I weave in a quotation into a story, weaving is just what it is — that is, the quotation should become part of the story, integrated into it, an interwoven pattern. In a novel, on the other hand, quotations should provide a contrast — it's a different life hanging there in the middle of this new life you are depicting.

In your stories you rather often use a male narrator, and of course you take the same approach in **The Slynx.**

Male or female makes no difference to me. I'm not

writing in the first-person masculine, after all, but in the third person. I'd never use the first person. I simply describe the life of a man, and then of a woman — sometimes through his eyes, sometimes through hers. It's all the same to me, really, because what is important is that it is a human being who sees all this. Inside a human being there is no gender. The soul doesn't have a gender. In the social, sexual, and various other senses there is gender, but the soul has none. Sometimes it's more convenient, quite simply, to look at everything from a particular point of view. In *The Slynx*, for example, the hero is a man because that gives him more freedom of movement, so it's convenient to look through his eyes. Also, he has to be a kind of fool and ignoramus. With a woman as a fool you have fewer narrative options — her social life is curtailed as it is. Women have the home, and that's about it. As for men, they assume that they own the whole world — they have science, and art, and philosophy, and work, and anything you like, so they are in contact with all sorts of different layers of life. And consequently they don't understand a single one of them. That is, it was more interesting and convenient that way, because you can send them to different places more often.

Creating the linguistic world of **The Slynx** *was a literary feat. How did you work at it? Did you borrow a lot from folklore?*

I needed a language that was unliterary and literary at the same time. The hardest thing was to mix in a certain amount of this unliterary color — from folklore, from rural and urban speech. It's not the language of folklore, but rather colloquial street language. So to mix in a sufficient amount to color the prose, but at the same time not so much that it becomes dense and stylized, because I really don't like it when it's too stylized. So what kind of things did I use? A small number of neologisms — I used mostly distorted versions of already existing words, but there are just a few neologisms — ten or fifteen, maybe, not more. Then there are corruptions of literary language — the language of ignorant, uneducated people who misunderstand the words. They associate them with folk etymologies. And then there are some verb forms that I borrowed from our nanny. We had a nanny from the Pskov province, where they speak a slightly different dialect. Some old forms have been preserved there, so I used them. And then there is the language of the correspondence between Ivan the Terrible and Prince Kurbsky. It's from the sixteenth century — another language, a different historical Russian that you need a translation to read. But there is a good edition that contains both the original and a translation. When you look at it you begin to understand, because it's a different grammatical system, and there are certain syntactic forms that aren't used any more, but they are interesting. I didn't analyze these texts linguistically but merely read a lot of them to get a feeling for their verve and density — Ivan the Terrible was an impetuous writer. He switches suddenly from one subject to another, and this is reflected in the syntax. It's like when someone doesn't finish what he is saying or doesn't finish his thought, and the thought dashes on, because some feeling wells up — here he starts to say something, and suddenly he feels insulted, remembers some offense, and bam! — he's already saying something else, about that insult. These thoughts dashing after feelings — it's such a clutter, such sloppiness, so unstructured. Figuring out how all this is done was very interesting.

And the result is a strange contrast between the style and the theme. We are simultaneously taking part in a dynamic linguistic feast and the destruction of civilization.

I needed to maintain some such dynamics. But while you're writing you don't know how to do that. It is really impossible to understand what you are doing.

What about now? When did you last read **The Slynx** *yourself?*

Probably about two years ago. There was some reprint or other, and I simply read the galleys. But I try to avoid reading my works for a long time, so that I can forget them myself and read them with a fresh eye. I was so worn out that I couldn't see what I'd written, because as I was writing at the same time I had to keep remembering what I'd written earlier in order not to repeat things, and, as they say, not become blind to my own text. I couldn't do that any longer. I needed to move the action along. Balancing the whole time is hard — like a snowball...

Literature in your works does not offer salvation. "Mice are our Mainstay" is the slogan in your novel. Not education, not books?

No, although that would seem to be a controversial thesis, because throughout my life and all during the sixties and seventies and even earlier, there was always this Old European view of things: enlightenment will help; if people learn what is good and what is bad they will become good; there is such a thing as progress; it's enough to bring them up right and educate them and they will be good. But then all that began to break down. It broke down throughout the whole twentieth century, and it turned out that all those wonderful well brought up people weren't like that at all.

For example, Communism here in Russia — well, it wasn't Communism but the Soviet regime which is not the same thing at all. When it began to draw to an end and break up, a lot of people had the illusion that all problems would be solved now — good books, good texts, and the people would immediately become intelligent and better, because all this had been concealed from them and now everything would be accessible. But what happened was exactly the opposite. Take book publishing. There are so many books published now! The bookstores are literally bursting with books — an endless flood of them, but the people are more and more stupid; they choose the worst books and don't want anything to do with good ones, and the circulation of the serious literary journals has shrunk to nothing. Take, for example, *Novy Mir* back in the late eighties — three million copies a year! Today it's three thousand. And thank heaven if you have that much. So where have they all gone, all these people who wanted to read?! They don't want to any more; it means nothing to them. They either don't read at all or have switched to doing something else. It turns out people don't need it at all. Earlier they would read a book like someone who, you know, sits there in a village in the wintertime and watches television because there isn't anything else to do. They would also read books, because there wasn't anything else to do. But now many people don't need books at all — they play sports, they race around in cars. That's where they get their enjoyment.

And they work so hard!

Yes, they work very hard. When you're tired you're not receptive — literature is so different from your work. But even those who don't have to work don't read. There aren't many people in the whole wide world who really need literature, if you think about it. Although there is some potential. In America, for example — I don't know Europe very well — but in America a lot of good books are published. Not necessarily great literature but there are some remarkable books of investigative journalism.

Yes. I don't think there's any of that in Russia.

None. We have the genre, but it's pop journalism — not serious. Writers don't want to really immerse themselves in their material. They don't want to work through this material and know it inside out and convey it properly. They want to show themselves. Here it's very, very underdeveloped.

Still, here **The Slynx** *became a bestseller.*

Yes.

And you received the Triumph Prize.

Well, yes.

You worked on the novel a lot while you were in the United States. Did being far from home help?

Yes and no. Sometimes you have to get away completely in order to write in peace, simply to get away from it all. On the other hand, you have to hear the language at home, because when you are outside Russia you begin to forget some aspects of the language. Your language — the literary, educated language — is still there, but you don't hear street language, because there are no Russian streets there. And this is very important — you walk down the street and you hear something and you think — aha! So this helps a lot. But over there you're in literary and linguistic isolation. I only know street language from what I hear — I don't speak it. While I was traveling a lot of new words came along that I still don't know how to use.

Over the course of many years I read with great pleasure your articles in various serious American journals. I just reread your amusing and frightening article **Russian Roulette,** *which you evidently haven't even published in Russian. It seems more like an essay than a social or political article. How do you see these texts?*

No, I haven't published them in Russian. There's no sense in doing that. I've only published one article — no, two — that I wrote for the American press in Russian, but I rewrote them. It's a different audience. It's one thing when you write for *The New York Review of Books* — that's also very difficult, because you're writing for people about whom you know very little — what kind of people they are, what they know, what has to be explained to them. Some things that you can do in Russian with a single word or even just hint at — say, for example, that you refer to Pushkin and you say: "Pushkin." You don't have to explain it. But over there you have to write "Pushkin, the great Russian poet." You have to explain things; you have to consider the whole time that they might not know something. I can't just leave something out — I have to explain why I've left it out or replace it with some other phrase. So I'm writing for an unknown audience. American intellectuals, I imagine.

These are your colleagues there at the university!

Yes, but not only — not only Slavists. And even my Slavist colleagues don't know anything — even they know nothing! I've been to various Slavist conferences — such incredible narrowness! Everyone works on their period, everyone works on their own thing. There are some very, very intelligent people there, but for some reason they dig in and don't want to listen to anything. If you tell them, "What you say here is wrong, it's not true." No, they will defend their turf. I'd rather write in Russian for a Russian audience.

As for now, what are you planning to write in Russian?

I have various projects going. I write very slowly, so I can't do everything that I'd like. There are people who sit down and write and it turns out wonderfully! But I can't do that — I do all this very slowly!

After returning to Russia you became a "show woman" hosting the popular **School of Slander** *that was awarded the Teffi[11] prize for the best talk show of 2004. But then comes the question "why Tolstaya — practically a modern classic — should indulge in these cruel amusements?"*

Ha, ha, ha!

That's what they wrote about you. The question remains.

It's interesting — there's your answer. Why interesting? Well, because I'm just made that way: I like to try different things, I find it interesting, for example, to talk on live TV with real live people. This is an enriching inner experiment, so to speak. I don't go to those in-crowd get-togethers — presentations, receptions — never. Never! Once or twice in my life I've been to them because I had to meet someone. It is such an unbearable, stupid way to spend time that I either start to feel hysterical, or I wish to fall asleep, just to avoid looking at it all! Nevertheless, hundreds and thousands of people go to such events and think that it's as normal as dropping into a store to buy a bread roll. So as to your question about why I'm doing what I'm doing, I can say that it gives

---

[11] Teffi (Nadezhda Aleksandrovna Lokhvitskaya 1872 – 1952) – Russian writer and poet known for her satirical poetry and feuilletons, especially those carried by the journal *Satirikon*. In 1920 she emigrated to Paris.

me living contact with people. So who needs this meaningless wandering around and exchanging glances and noticing who's dressed in what and munching on sandwiches or whatever — why waste your life on that?! Why?! Yet that's how ninety percent of our in-crowd lives — writers, television people, fluttering like butterflies from flower to flower. It's terrible! At these gatherings you won't see a single real live person! And how are you going to see one otherwise? I have a few friends. Where am I going to get new ones? Am I supposed to go out on the street to meet them? No. Besides everything else, I need contact with other real live people. Contact through conversation, because you question them, you ask them direct, indirect, provocative questions, and depending on how they behave when they answer, they kind of take shape as individuals: can they cope with the questions, can they or can't they cope — I give them every opportunity. Different people handle it differently. People define themselves when they argue, and that's interesting. It's interesting to examine people as individuals — interesting! As for mixing with the crowd, that's not at all interesting. That's why the show is important to me. There are all sorts of circumstances involved here. I was thinking of leaving a long time ago, and now I think I'll work this year out and then quit.

It must take quite a lot of time.

No, that's not why. Before it took a lot of energy, but then I got used to it. It's just not as interesting any more, quite simply. The same situations repeat themselves, people begin to repeat themselves, questions get the same answers. On the one hand, the material has dwindled. On the other, there aren't enough people interesting to me who would agree to come. Some just don't want to, while others can't for various reasons; it doesn't fit their schedule — it never does. And the censorship is awful! The television censorship is monstrous — people are afraid to say what they think. Who needs their cautious answers?! You're no longer really talking with people.

Let's return to the question of whether a soul has gender. A critic wrote in Ex Libris *recently: "There is no respect in our society for women's prose, just as there is none for female logic or women drivers." It seems to me that you personally have escaped being defined like that, but do you think that attitudes on this subject are changing?*

This is something on an entirely different level. For example, there is a myth — at one time it was not a myth, but now it is — that there is such a thing as a specifically feminine prose. But that is a working hypothesis. Take the nineteenth century: few women were writing, for a thousand different reasons; they were limited socially — they didn't have passports, they couldn't do anything without their husbands' or fathers' permission. It was different in different countries — in Europe, in Russia, everywhere it was different: in some places they could inherit, in others they couldn't. So women were forbidden some things and not permitted others. So here comes women's emancipation, — suffragettes, various feminisms, women's emancipation in general from this, that, and the other. Good. So women have been emancipated. On the one hand, it's impossible just to up and emancipate from everything. What are you being emancipated from — children? The kitchen? From your feminine essence, as it were — you can't be emancipated from that! You can attain a certain level of social equality; that is, you can be paid equally for equal work, and that would be good, if it were that way. You can do some other things, but some things you can't do at all! Why should you be equal to men — you're different! You are utterly different!

And as a writer? A woman first, and only then a writer?

The thing is that some myths are useful for various political ends. There are different kinds of feminism: according to one kind, women and men are not at all different from each other, whereas another maintains on the contrary that they are so different that everything about them is different, including prose. And this notion that women's prose is different comes from this political myth. Well, perhaps bad women's prose is different from bad men's prose, just as men are different from women. But if the prose is genuine, then to that extent it makes no difference whether it was written by a man or a woman. Lev Tolstoy's story *Kholstomer* is about a horse. Was he ever a horse?! He was never a horse! In, say, *Anna Karenina* he described a woman's soul better than any woman in the history of literature. In the whole history of literature no woman has described a woman's soul like that! Especially before Tolstoy. After him, I don't know — Sigrid Undset, for example, is a wonderful writer, but Tolstoy wrote before her and already knew how to see and write about some things. In that respect he influenced everyone a great deal. But he was the first in Europe to describe a woman's soul like that — with such subtlety! So on a high level, so to speak, there really is no gender. On a low one, however, there is, because on the whole, women are more apt to pay attention to details. This is good in good prose and very bad in bad prose. Men are more inclined toward abstract concepts, which is also very bad in bad prose.

But am I right in saying that you have been spared such labels?

Not everywhere. We didn't have this at all earlier —

this very marginal notion that there is such a thing as women's prose — and I have always rejected it. But when we started getting all these contacts with all sorts of women's movements and women's conferences and European fairs, certain critics just decided: "Aha, this is the latest fashion from Europe! They're wearing it there, so we'll wear it here and look at everything from this angle." For heaven's sake go right ahead! All of these studies are utterly marginal. There's a lot of room for idiots there. There are also profound, interesting things to study, but all the idiots have rushed in — it's an easy way to make a living! So in some contexts they put me in women's prose. I occasionally take part in different round tables and conferences, but it's impossible — again about women! Again about women! I'm endlessly invited to different round tables, but I don't go. They are starting to use me, they want to use me, you understand, in situations that are entirely alien to me! Here just recently in Moscow there was a world economic forum, and they wanted me to come and sit at a round table and talk about women's achievements in literature. Why? I wrote to them that I am a writer, not an economist. I can't add two and two and get the same answer every time. Do you understand — that's not what I do! And whether you're a man or a woman has nothing to do with it. Women earn money in literature not because they're women, but because people buy or don't buy their books — it's a commercial matter. Marinina earns more than anyone: she can afford to build herself multistory palaces — thank God! She's a woman. Some men also earn a lot. The rest of them not much.

When I interviewed you three or four years ago you were active politically, and that's almost an exception among Russian writers. What about now?

There isn't any politics any more. Politics is over. There's simply no political life to speak of, so I don't take part in anything any more. It's interesting to participate in an honest competition, but when all the places have been bought beforehand, it's not interesting at all. That's it.

That's sad.

Yes, it's sad, sad. Sad and frightening, and no one knows what's next. Everyone is predicting all sorts of bad things. All the analysts — serious and otherwise — everyone is saying that all this is not going to end well.

Ludmila ULITSKAYA

"By training I'm a geneticist. In a certain sense I haven't changed professions but merely research methods and tools".

A. Sazonov

Ludmila Yevgenyevna Ulitskaya was born on 23 February 1943 in the town of Davlekanovo in the Autonomous Republic of Bashkiria, where her family had been evacuated from Moscow during WWII. She graduated from Moscow State University with a degree in biology. A geneticist by training, she worked for two years at the Institute of General Genetics at the Russian Academy of Sciences but was dismissed in 1970 for reproducing samizdat.

In 1979-82 she worked as literary director of the Chamber Jewish Theater. She wrote sketches, children's plays, dramatizations for radio and children's and puppet theaters, reviewed plays, and translated poetry.

Ulitskaya began publishing stories in the journals in the late 1980s. Her scripts for the films *Liberty Sisters* (*Sestrichki Liberti*; 1990) directed by Vladimir Grammatikov and *A Woman for Everybody* (*Zhenshchina dlya vsekh*; 1991) directed by Anatoly Mateshko and her novella *Sonechka* (*Novy mir*, 1992) brought her wide recognition. In 1994 this novella won the

French Medici Prize for the best translated work of the year. It was also in France and in French that her first book — the collection *Poor Relatives* (*Bednye rodstvenniki*) — appeared. In 1997 she was a Booker Prize finalist for her novel *Medea and Her Children* (*Medeya i ee deti*), and in 2001 she received the Russian Booker for her novel *The Kukotsky Case* (*Kazus Kukotskogo*). Her novel *Sincerely Yours, Shurik* (*Iskrenne vash Shurik*) was a 2004 bestseller. In 2006 Ulitskaya published *Daniel Stein, Interpreter* (*Daniel Shtain, perevodchik*) a novel based on real events. Her works have been translated into twenty-five languages.

Today it's difficult to believe that you were first published abroad. Is that really true, or is it just a story?

It's quite an amazing story, but my first book did indeed come out in France, in French, with Gallimard. Just a little ahead of the Russian edition, but it's a fact. An even more surprising fact given that this was the only time Gallimard ever published a translated book by a writer who still hadn't published a book at home. There was a confluence of happy circumstances: I gave the manuscript of *Poor Relations* (*Bednye rodstvenniki*) to my friend Masha Zonina, a French translator, and she gave it to a colleague of hers who had been working for many years with Gallimard, and this colleague in turn sent it off with a positive recommendation to the publishers, who also reviewed it, and I got a contract in the mail. I know that such things happen only in bad movie scripts, but that's exactly how it was — a modern Cinderella story.

You must be one of those people who are constantly writing. When and how did you begin to write in earnest?

I think I began writing as soon as I'd learned to write — very early. As a child I wrote poetry, and I even do so occasionally today. I kept diaries, wrote letters, and notes. There were always scribbled scraps of paper in my pockets and bag and desk. I chose to become a biologist, studied genetics, and if they hadn't kicked me out of my job I probably wouldn't have changed professions, because I found it very interesting. I didn't work for almost ten years, and then after this long pause went to work in the Jewish theater, in charge of the literary section. That was adventurous on my part. After three years, in 1982, I left it and since then I've been a professional writer. During the '80s I did all sorts of literary work — animated film scripts and reviews, I translated poetry, wrote screenplays for educational television programs, did dramatizations and plays for puppet and children's theater. My first short stories appeared in print in the late '80s. And it took off from there.

Could you have become a writer if the Soviet Union still existed?

That's difficult to say. Perhaps I could have. The thing is that I was an "extra-Soviet" writer. I've always been interested in the private person, in his or her ability to survive in society, whereas for me politics has always been an unavoidable evil. I can state very confidently that I would never have become a "Soviet" writer.

In the short story The Corridor System (Koridornaya sistema) eight-year-old Zhenya reads Don Quixote, and I assume you also read all the classics when you were quite young. As for Soviet literature, what did you read and how did it affect you?

I very much liked Boris Zhitkov's *What I Saw (Chto ya*

videl) — it's a wonderful children's book — and I was right about him as a writer. A few years ago I read a novel of his about the Russian Revolution. The plates were destroyed at the typesetter's in 1937 but by some miracle the work survived. It came out a couple of years ago, and it turns out that Zhitkov really is a splendid writer. As a child I read everything on the curriculum. In the upper classes it included Soviet literature on a standardized reading list — Ostrovsky's *How the Steel Was Tempered*, Fadeev's *Young Guard* (*Molodaya gvardiya*), later on Mayakovsky. The main thing wasn't whether these books were good or bad, but that they were recommended ideological models, and that set me against them. I was so disgusted with the mind-numbing teaching methods and literature at school that it wasn't until afterwards that I could read the Russian classics with fresh eyes. But I managed to make some of my own discoveries. When I was thirteen I discovered Boris Pasternak, and for a long time I thought that no one knew him besides me. Later I learned to my astonishment that a schoolgirl friend of mine knew him in the flesh, because she also lived in the Peredelkino writers' village and would say hello to him on the street. Amazing! I was very prejudiced, and I suspected that Soviet literature was non-existent. But then I discovered Andrei Platonov and the great poetry that was alive in spite of the iron regime. Of course there was Trifonov, and Nagibin, and Kazakov, but I passed them by out of childish snobbery.

You have said many times that you did not have any literary models, yet you often mention Nabokov, Chekhov, and others with great respect.

It would never occur to me to call these great writers my teachers. The distance is too great. In general I don't think it's my business to look into who has influenced me. In my childhood, however, I was carried away in turns by various writers, "falling in love" with O'Henry, then Bunin…. My last passion, when I was already at the university, was Nabokov… it was really strong for many years. Then *Ada* turned me off. But again I want to stress that I'd never dare call myself a pupil of these great writers.

This isn't the first time we meet. Do you remember what you said about "perestroika," about "restructuring"? You said that you didn't have to restructure anything in your family, because you had no illusions…

Right. Both of my grandfathers went to prison. They knew the regime for what it was. The older generation kept quiet and didn't tell us much, but their fear and disgust leached through. Many people were in the grip of such feelings. So I didn't have to restructure my attitude to the surrounding world when the Soviet Union collapsed, and I feel even less need for it today. I've known for a long time that there is a conflict between the private individual and the state. It's always there, even in the most decent states. The state always tries to make all its citizens into convenient subjects, and citizens taken individually try as hard as they can to preserve their identity, their individuality, if you will. It's an existential conflict. Under totalitarianism, however, it descends from the existential level to the level of genocide. Everyone has illusions, of course. I also had a lot of them that had nothing to do with the nature of power.

Professional competence in fields other than literature always seems to be a great asset for a writer. You grew up in a family of doctors and have medical training. What has it meant to you as a writer?

I think that it's indeed important for writers to have a "second" education. Moreover, I don't understand what a "literary" education is supposed to be. My training is not in medicine but the natural sciences, which is quite close. Moscow University and the Department of Genetics, where I got my degree, gave me a great deal. When life is your object of study, you expand your consciousness. An object looking at an object. And then you also feel a deep kinship with mice, fish, and sweet peas, because the unified structure of the world shows through. Genetics, more than any other science, knows how closely related all higher education in the humanities is, and I constantly feel the lack. The sad thing is that I'm aware that so many important elements of culture elude me, and there's no time any more to learn.

Do you think it is your educational background that has enabled you to portray eroticism so naturally — beginning already with **Sonechka***?*

To answer your question I'll have to digress very far from the specific point you're asking about.

I don't think that the intellectual and physiological spheres are separate. The erotic is equally physiological and intellectual. Human beings are whole beings, and the very intent to determine what is "high" and "low" in humans is a product of our skewed, imperfect civilization, where this divide has existed for centuries. "It" has become a hush zone, a taboo area, and a very important part of human existence remains in this hush zone.

Actually, the question as I see it is quite different: how to write about "it"? The Russian language is very chaste — it doesn't even have a literary vocabulary for amorous themes. All we have are medical terms, the unusable dirty words, not included in any academic dictionaries, or euphemisms. Writing about delicate, very intimate experiences with such philological resources is a challenge.

When I began writing I didn't theorize. Overall I rely less on constructs and concepts than on experiences and emotions. Even the intellectual aspect is colored emotionally. This is neither good nor bad — it's all a question of inner organization.

When I was writing *Sonechka* I was rather distant from the cultural anthropological topics that I've become more and more interested in as time goes on. Eroticism attracted me not because of the taboo in Russian literature that has now been partially canceled, but because it was a weakly developed theme. I don't have any ambition to exhaust this theme, but I'd like to find a "legitimate" way of getting it out in the open, at least in part, as much as possible. I think I did as much as I could in *Sincerely Yours, Shurik*. I'm not likely to do any better, although my earlier novels, *Medea and her Children* and *The Kukotsky Case,* deal with certain aspects of human eroticism as well.

Physiology is simply the means by which human and animal bodies function, and satisfying the human sexual drive is as legitimate as the process of digestion. Human neural activity and social motivation are very complex, however, and an enormous number of cultural prohibitions are not established once and for all but change over time, sometimes very traumatically. But this is the purview of science, not of art. As for me, I dare to hope that I will remain in art, but I came to it with everything I knew before, in my biological past.

I remember that in **Medea** *children are put on the potty. This must be a first in Russian literature?*

No, what are you talking about! What about Natasha

Rostova and the dirty diaper in the final chapters of *War and Peace*? For a long time the critics took this diaper as a symbol of Tolstoy's lack of respect for women, but you and I both know that a dirty diaper is something very important for anyone raising a child.

You address all the themes that were more or less forbidden in Soviet literature: eroticism, sexual minorities, abortion, alcoholism, the disabled, diseases, and of course death. Do you see yourself in any way as a pioneer?

Quite honestly, I've never thought about it. There was so much bustling around me that abounded in people's life stories. These stories simply overwhelmed me — there was so much interesting life going on, such dramas, such exploits and such treachery! It never occurred to me to use any filters, even less so in the case of death. Without death there is no life, for it is death that gives everything meaning and value. It wouldn't have helped to try to close my eyes to this fact or avoid the theme, because it inevitably comes to everyone. Death is nearby the whole time, and it is what gives moments of joy their intensity and makes us value love. We don't know what secret we may discover after death. I think that everyone's death is meant for them alone, but if love does exist in the afterlife, it must be something entirely different from what we call love here on earth. Atheists must forgive me if I seem to be destroying their beliefs, but I don't think any atheist would be disappointed to find a new space beyond earthly life.

Actually, much more than speculating on what awaits us beyond death, I'm interested in this threshold boundary itself — in the dying, the departure. I have witnessed wonderful departures by wonderful people. But I've also seen other, no less wonderful people suffer horribly as they died.

There is yet another essential point — in literature I felt like a dilettante, and this gave me an enormous sense of freedom. I wasn't obligated to anyone for anything; because no one had given or granted me a thing. I did what I liked and the way I could. I didn't expect to succeed, and that gave me an additional degree of freedom.

In *The Funeral Party (Vesyolye pokhorony)* you even use Alik's dying to illustrate the cultural difference between Russia and America.

Yes. I was struck in America by the fact that people usually die in medical institutions rather than at home among their families. In Russia until recently this was not the custom — everyone wanted to die in the bosom of their family, not in a hospital. Our very poor hospitals are one sad reason, but that's just on the surface. I think there is a deeper reason. American civilization is so focused on success and prosperity that people don't want thoughts of death to disturb their good mood or keep them from enjoying life, whereas life in Russia doesn't let you forget about death. I don't want to elaborate on this theme here, because it would inevitably take us out of a philosophical discussion into social problems.

People have suddenly appeared in your novels and short stories that simply did not exist in Soviet literature: Jews, different ethnic groups, homosexuals, the disabled, mentally retarded, the poor — those who are most hidden from view. How did you find them?

I've already mentioned that very early on I started thinking about who stands up best under the crush of power, and I made a discovery — a small one, but my very own: people who are not trying to succeed. Those who want to be winners in this life inevitably lose the contours of their individuality. People on the margins with no ambition to win a better place preserve their selves. That's where my heroes are: the nurse Medea, who doesn't pursue a career and wants to stay in the shadows but doesn't yield anything to the authorities and at a critical moment in her life is not afraid to act according to her conscience. Her husband failed at his career because despite all his revolutionary ideas he was unable to take part in an execution and fainted. "My organism couldn't take it!" he says. Those who have nothing to lose — the poor and the invalids — are not afraid of the Soviet regime because they have already lost everything. Theirs is the special courage of the outcasts. And I don't go looking for them, our life is full of them.

Toward the end of **The Through Line (Skvoznaya liniya)** *we meet the Chechen woman Violetta, surely one of the very rare positive portraits of a Chechen in contemporary Russian literature?*

Possibly. I'm often criticized for writing about the 1970s and '80s and ignoring the present. So here a Chechen woman came into sight, just as it happened in real life. I really like the fact that people are so different. I remember that the first time I was in the New York subway, I almost cried from joy. The culture itself seemed to have switched polarities — this "Babylon" that has always been regarded as an unholy mélange of peoples, a cultural abomination, looked so wonderful! People of all colors, in different clothes, reading newspapers in different languages, all joined together by the same music… There were all sorts of people in my class at the university: a Korean girl, an Ossetian, a Latvian, not to mention a Cuban, a Somali, and a Venezuelan. We found each other interesting, and there wasn't a trace of racism among us. But today Russia has become a racist country full of hatred for blacks, Asians, and Caucasians, not to mention Jews. We're signing our own death warrant.

Let's talk some more about human dignity. You show it in the process of development — not only Pavel Alekseevich defying Stalin's laws, but also Sonechka ironing a tablecloth or Medea cooking for her many relatives.

It's nice to be understood correctly, because it means that to some extent I've been able to pass on the lesson that I learned from my grandmother. I loved her very much, but it wasn't until I was older that I understood how respected she was. She was a woman of rare dignity: I never heard her raise her voice. Her sense of her own dignity obliged her to act in an extraordinarily dignified manner, and this code included not only fulfilling obligations, but fulfilling them in the best way possible. I was always impatient and sloppy. My grandmother would be so sincerely surprised at seeing carelessness that you became uncomfortable. During the war she would wash our white tablecloth, even though you had to bring water from the river, and on top of that in the winter. But she was convinced that you shouldn't let yourself go to the point that you ate off a newspaper. And all they had to eat was millet. There were quite a few people like that in my grandmother's generation, and I remember them with gratitude.

And yet you are still accused of writing on "trivial themes"?

Yes, they've said that as well. Now it seems they've stopped. But I don't want to give the impression that everything written about me in Russia is negative. I must say that there are many positive reviews and large editions of my books —

this year the total has topped a million copies. And there are readers for whom what I do is important.

I think that on the contrary, out of these so-called trivial themes a big theme grows. I mean everyday family life, and the family itself as a haven and protection.

Much more. The family as the world, as the universe. And perhaps even my former profession has taught me something — heredity through biochemistry, through DNA, which is to a greater or lesser extent subject to Mendel's laws, and social heredity, which runs through the family, through moral influence and upbringing.

Your idea of the family is thus connected with traditions and decency? The family as the savior or guarantee of inner freedom?

Like the institution of marriage, the institution of the family is undergoing a serious crisis. For me the family is connected with certain traditions; it is the child's first defense against a hostile society, the source of support and nourishment. But life often shows us something entirely different as well. To understand what a bad family is, all you have to do is look at a juvenile correctional center. More than half the children serving time there for more or less serious offenses are victims of their own families.

Many times you have described the story of a single family over the course of almost a century. Why do you need such a perspective?

It is above all the family that anchors the individual in the world. Disrupted family ties are a disaster. In Russia, which has been at war continuously since the Russo-Japanese campaign early in the 20th century, the family has been under constant threat. The broken family is a sign of a broken world.

It is through the family that we apprehend the basis of life, and nothing can replace the family in that role. People without families run wild, whereas those who grow up in good, loving families establish better ties with the surrounding world. The family itself is a model of the world. The Biblical stories my great-grandfather used to tell me seemed like the story of our family. This is how we become linked to history and culture.

You yourself are a representative of two religious traditions — Jewish and Orthodox. What does this mean to you as a writer?

That's a very, very difficult question. First of all, it's important to me not so much as a writer, but as a human being. It's sort of like having two professions, in that it allows you to see the world from two points of view. There were times when I appeared to have a problem of choice here. Now as I'm getting on in years it no longer seems that way, all the more so since I've had a glimpse into another tradition, namely Buddhism. This has also been a fruitful experience. The Abrahamic religions appear to be very rigid. Today I think that Judeo-Christian culture has a great deal to learn from tolerance as practiced in the East. The aggressiveness typical of the Christian world, the ferocious conviction that it has the one and only truth in its pocket, bears bitter fruit. How the Holocaust could occur in the bosom of Christian civilization is a question that has no answer.

Also, I must confess something else: I am no longer interested at all in dogmatic theology — not the Trinity, or the Virgin Birth, or even the fundamental question of whether the Savior was truly God, or the Son of God, or a great teacher and prophet. All that interests me is behavior — how people treat their neighbors. It doesn't even matter to me very much what they think.

The amount of cruelty in the world is beyond imagination, and no religious tradition can change anything.

Let's talk about your life in Russia as a writer. Western critics were immediately well disposed toward you, but Russian critics were quite severe. They spoke of "ladies' literature," and "sentimental women's novels," and so on. They praised the precision and beauty of your language, but they didn't like your themes.

I think that the difference in the critical assessments of my books in the West and in Russia reflects the anti-woman bias of Russian males more than it does any objective parameters. It has less to do with the nature of my writing than with the nature of our society, which contains a profound paradox. Traditionally and historically Russia is an Eastern country in the sense that women have always been second-rate citizens. On the other hand, the demographics here are such that in the twentieth century women have always far outnumbered men. During the incessant revolutions and wars throughout the century, women took responsibility for both military production and agriculture. Men always remained the leaders, and this order of things has persisted right down to the present. There are extremely few women in the leadership, their number in parliament is negligible, and their influence in society insignificant. There is only one women's organization of any authority or significance, and that's the Committee of Soldiers' Mothers.

There are many remarkable women's names in today's culture, but the majority of artists, writers, and musicians are undoubtedly men. Probably only in the performing world proper — the cinema, the theater — do women enjoy the same rights as men. At any rate I've never heard anyone say "What a good actress, even if she is a woman!"

Today it seems to me that it is the level of culture that determines how much women participate in the life of the country. Everything I've said, of course, applies only to Europe and America. The Islamic world lives by completely different laws, and I'm not about to judge whether they are good or bad, since millions of people are quite satisfied with the parameters of their civilization.

In our critics' constant attempts to divide literature into men's and women's I've always sensed unconscious discrimination. There are every bit as many bad books written by men as by women. Often, even when I'm being praised, this demeaning nuance is there — "Ulitskaya writes well, almost like a man!"

As a former geneticist I can assure you that everything that men and women do they do a little differently. They have different physiologies, different hormonal balances, and different psyches. Men and women are called upon to live as partners in this world, however, and I'm convinced that broader participation by women in all areas of social life would help to mitigate cruelty, temper aggression, and reform social programs to benefit children and the poorest classes of society.

I write the way only a woman can write — with a woman's view of the world and about problems women understand — and I don't try to make my books more "masculine." Quite a few of my readers are men. (By the way, according to the statistics, 70% of all book readers are women!)

I try not to hurry, I try to be honest and independent, including independent of the critics.

In 2001 you won the Russian Booker Prize. What did or perhaps does this mean to you?

Most of all the Booker Prize changed my position in the market by increasing sales. I was of course very glad to get it. More important to me, however, is that my books have made the short list three times, because this says more about quality than a one-time victory. The thing is that giving out prizes always involves some extra-literary considerations. For example, Ludmila Petrushevskaya didn't get the prize for an excellent novel that made the short list. Instead it went to a book that I think can't be compared with hers on any basis. Her novel *Number One, or in the Gardens of Other Opportunities (Nomer odin, ili v sadu drugikh vozmozhnostey)* was probably too complex even for the jury. I think that if a work equal in stature to Kafka's *The Trial* or Joyce's *Ulysses* were to be written today, it wouldn't have much of a chance. All the literary prizes suffer from too much democratism, and even with the most objective jury there's always an element of the lottery. For that reason I don't have any illusions about my successes. Prizes far from always reflect the real state of things in literature.

Individual people in your novels are at the forefront, while historical and political events are in the background — even far in the background. In **The Kukotsky Case,** *for example, personal and moral things are much more important than Stalin's policies.*

The State is an extra-moral category. Its function is to defend, to manage, to distribute. The ideology it creates may be quite immoral, like Nazism in Germany and Communism in the USSR. When the social ideology is immoral, it can be confronted only by individuals. And that is my theme — the confrontation between the individual and the State. By coming out against the social morality of a given time and place the individual implements his or her notion of freedom, conscience, and morality. Doctor Kukotsky is one of those people who could not come to terms with what he considered unjust. The evil he encountered was completely impersonal in form, but his position was deeply personal, and perhaps in some respect mistaken as well.

You give much consideration to abortion as a moral question, but there doesn't seem to be any answer.

I don't have an answer. In the poorest countries where there isn't any contraception or abortion — India, for example — we see women giving birth to children, and almost half of them die in infancy from hunger and disease. I don't think that abortion is a greater evil than the suffering of a baby doomed to die of starvation. Doctor Kukotsky, the hero of my novel, continually encounters situations in which women have illegal abortions and die, leaving their living, already existing children orphans. And he thinks that abortions should be allowed.

What do I think about all this personally? Abortion is a great misfortune for a woman, a profound shock that produces great moral stress. Still, I think that it is the woman who should make the decision, not the Pope in Rome or Stalin, if only because the Pope is a man and a monk, and I don't consider Stalin a paragon of morality. Let me add, incidentally, that one human life is neither more nor less precious than another.

Could you comment on how social changes in recent years have affected your work?

Not at all.

But I see one change — in Sincerely Yours, Shurik *you begin writing about eroticism in a different way...*

Please note that I began this novel before any of my other books. I jotted down the first notes connected with *Shurik* in the early '80s, before I had even touched *Medea*. I wrote it over the course of twenty years, with long interruptions. I think that I myself and my attitude toward the theme changed a lot during these years. I don't know about other writers, but the books I write change me. I even seem to get a little wiser in the process.

What would you like to be called — a woman writer or merely a writer?

I think that you have to observe the laws of the language you speak. Since Russian has a feminine form of the word for "writer" — *pisatelnitsa* as opposed to the masculine *pisatel* — people can call me that. I hope that the difference is purely grammatical.

What do you find most positive in Russian literature today?

Surprising as it may seem, it's in literature that I see the most talent and freedom. Circumstances today are such that state censorship has once again appeared in television and the mass media. So far literature has not been censored, and it is very diverse — as indeed it should be. Major events include Ruben Gallego's *White on Black* (*Beloye na chyornom*), Ludmila Petrushevskaya's *Number One, or in the Garden of Other Opportunities*. New writers, young and colorful, are appearing all the time. All's well.

Your latest novel, **Daniel Stein, Interpreter,** *is very different from your earlier prose with respect to both theme and structure. What happened?*

I've never been overly concerned with form — the story itself determines the style. In this particular case it gave me a lot of trouble, and I groped my way toward it. The published book is the third draft — I threw out the first two. From the very beginning I tried to write a documentary book. There is one such book in English about Rufeisen, the prototype of my hero, and another little one — a brochure, more or less — in German. I was very dissatisfied with both of them, because they both missed what was most essential, namely not only his war-time heroism but the heroism in his spiritual life as a priest. His renunciation of many of the Church's ideas and practices was also heroic, and that is what most fascinated me.

The documentary material proved to be very difficult. I couldn't handle it, couldn't find the right intonation. It wasn't until I got away from strict factuality by giving the hero a new name and introducing new characters that I began to get results. I had a lot of documents at my disposal, including statements by Daniel Rufeisen, and there were papers left by a certain Polish woman, a Communist. Some things I invented. I read a lot and consulted with many different people. So that's how the book took shape. One very difficult problem was montaging the documents, not unlike making a movie.

I wanted the author to be minimally present, or even better, completely absent. As it turned out, however, this didn't give enough color, so I added my letters to Yelena Kostyu-kovich as a kind of commentary on the entire work. I included five letters — in actual fact we wrote each other 900 during this period. Incidentally, this is an indication of the overall efficiency coefficient of the book. I think that for every page I wrote I read, studied, wrote, and discarded 200 pages. It was very difficult work. Today I don't even understand how I was able to do it.